HEAVEN ON EARTH

Martyn Croft

ISBN: 978-0-9559872-2-9

In this work of fiction, the characters, places and events are either the product of the author's imagination or they are used entirely fictitiously. Any resemblance to actual persons, living or dead, is purely coincidental.

Front cover photo: St Peter's Church, Trusthorpe

For Rachel, who has already started the journey

'He whom I wished to see,
Wished for to hear;
Where's all the joy and mirth,
Made life a heaven on earth?'

Lady Caroline Keppel (1735-?)

CONTENTS

1

Awakening

Edward Compton had been 'asleep' for just over two months, but it hadn't been a real sleep; it hadn't been caused by tiredness nor had it been a natural sleep. You see, Eddie was dead. Like his best friend Len, who had been tragically killed in a car crash a few months previously, shortly after moving with his family to Kent, Eddie too had met an untimely end but in rather more strange and unearthly circumstances. His sad demise had occurred in of all places, the Eternal City – a very appropriate appellation for the departure lounge for his escape from this world because, indeed, now Eddie had all eternity to look forward to. On the face of it, as far as their parents and families had been concerned and up to the time that he moved away, Leonard Wilby and Eddie had spent their early teenage years like any other boys growing up in the early sixties in a typical seaside town on the East Anglian coast. As far as the two best friends were concerned, nothing could have been further from the truth, given all the fantastic adventures they had been on involving time and space travel. Indeed, after Len's sad passing, Eddie, while still 'alive and kicking', had gained great comfort in also miraculously being part of the ghostly world which his late-departed friend had started to inhabit. Unfortunately, one such ghostly adventure had led Eddie to pass for 'real' into that ghostly world where he had previously only been a temporary observer.

"*C'mon, Captain, it's time to wake up!*"

A familiar voice echoed in Eddie's head, but all around him was still an all-enveloping blackness. The voice continued.

"*It's me, Eddie.*"

Eddie suddenly felt a warm glow within and the darkness seemed to lift as bright sunshine began to filter into his new world. He tried to speak.

"L-Len?"

Laughter.

"Got it in one, mate. Welcome to my world!"

Eddie's eyes flickered open and he began to take in his new surroundings. *'This isn't Rome'*, he thought as he tried desperately to recall his last living moments in the real world. Fortunately, any memory of his tragic end had been wiped from his mind 'forever'.

"Where am I?"

"Fenton-on-Sea, mate. Good old, boring Fenton."

Eddie looked around him. Now wide awake, he found himself sitting on a familiar bench on the promenade with the beautiful blue sea in front of him. Other sights registered themselves with him; the pier to his right, the lightship on the horizon and Len himself, standing smiling directly in front of him – all familiar reminders of his home town.

"How ...?"

Len finished Eddie's attempted question.

"How did you get here?"

"Y-yes."

Len looked sad and with a tinge of guilt etched lightly on his face, he said,

"I tried to stop you but you just didn't see it and …."

Eddie held up his hand – he didn't need to hear anymore. His response was brief.

"Don't, Len. Stop it!"

Len sat down bedside his best friend and put his arm round his fellow ghost; in so doing, neither of them felt anything physical.

"It's alright, Captain," said Len. "Look on the bright side. We can now see each other whenever we want and think of the other advantages."

"Such as?" asked Eddie.

"Well, for one, no one can see either of us now."

Eddie's mood seemed to lighten a little and Len continued.

"And we can go anywhere we want and when we want to as well."

The warm glow returned and Eddie began to feel an inner contentment beyond anything he had ever experienced in his real life. He felt safe and happy to be with his best friend again. What did he have to worry about? He wasn't going back to school; he wasn't going to have to take any more exams; he wasn't going to have to go to university or get a job and, above all, he wasn't going to die! He was going to 'live' forever, a contented fourteen-year-old, except ….

"What's up, Eddie?" asked Len seeing his friend apparently in deep thought.

"How old are we, Len?"

"Well, we *would* have both been fifteen now, mate."

"Fifteen?" asked a bemused Eddie. "But I was only fourteen when I …."

"Yes, but that was in January. Look around you, old son. It's high summer now and, anyway, we'd already moved forward to May when you had your unfortunate accident, so you could say that you were already fifteen then, although since our last time travel all happened on the same day, you could also say that you stayed as fourteen."

Eddie went quiet while he appeared to do some calculations.

"So really I've been dead for about six months in real time and it's the summer of 1966?"

"Yes, Captain, July 30th to be precise, but there's one thing you're forgetting."

"What's that?"

Len smiled warmly at his ghostly friend.

"We actually don't age, unless that is …."

"Unless?"

"Unless we want to, of course."

"We have that in our power, Len?"

"Who knows, old boy? Anything maybe possible in time. Just enjoy the ride, my friend – at the moment, you're fourteen and I'm fifteen. How long we've been dead is irrelevant; six months, a hundred years; it's all the same to us now, Ed."

Eddie ignored the shortened appellation of his name, even though Len never called him by it when they had been alive because, apart from the date seeming to jog something else in Eddie's memory, he was still frowning over the apparent conundrum – there was a problem with his calculations. He shared the puzzle with his friend.

"I left Fenton-on-Sea on January the 22nd, right?"

"Yes, if you say so," replied Len with a twinkle in his eye.

"But we had moved forward in time to late May when we went to Rome and so …."

"So you've only been dead for two months or so," said Len. "What does it matter?"

Eddie seemed satisfied with his friend's explanation but his mathematical and ordered mind would remain unhappy for some time with the apparent paradox – it appeared to him that he had 'lost' four months of time whether it was regarded as real or not. Of course, if Len was right, it really didn't matter as they weren't going to age anymore in the future, whatever that meant. Future, past, present – all might be mixed up in his new world.

While he was thinking on the matter, still sitting with head bowed, other voices abruptly entered Eddie's head.

"*Come on, dear, let's sit down; my feet are killing me.*"

"*Good idea, love; it's a bit too hot for a walk.*"

Eddie looked up to see not only Len with a cheeky smile on his face, but also an elderly man and woman looming over the promenade seat. The lady was just in the act of depositing her ample rear end directly on Eddie's lap, when he came to his senses with a start, even though he would never have felt any contact. Force of human habit caused him to jump upright and straight into Len's friendly but ghostly embrace and he then knew something was wrong. It wasn't just the lack of physical contact when he seemed to pass right through his friend's ethereal body and into the bright sunlight behind him. That sunlight should have been reflecting on a silver St Christopher round Len's neck; the St Christopher that his best friend had promised he would always wear, in life and death. Len's open-neck shirt could not disguise any such jewellery. Something was wrong. Turning back to face his friend's ghost, he asked quietly,

"Where's your St Christopher, Len?"

"*What did you say, my love?*"

"*Nothing, dear. I never said a word.*"

Len ushered Eddie a few yards down the promenade and out of earshot of the elderly couple who had obviously and strangely heard his friend's question. They walked side by side down onto the pebbly beach and on reaching the water's edge, Eddie repeated his query.

"I said: Where's your silver chain?"

"What sil …?"

Len didn't finish as he guessed that he'd been caught out. Eddie knew what he had to do next. After Len had died, they had developed a secret code to make sure of each other's identities when Len reappeared to Eddie in ghostly form. This exchange of codes had been vital in Len's case as his ghost could appear in different forms, both good and evil.

Eddie smiled and began to take control of the situation. He tried out the code.

"What a *blithe* day, comrade!"

Len looked nervous but tried to bluff his way through.

"Have you swallowed a dictionary, Captain?"

"Just like your mum's middle name, mate, but spelt with a 'Y'. Am I right?"

Eddie turned to look behind him. Immediately his eye was caught by a stab of bright white light as the strong sunshine glinted off a silver St Christopher hung round the neck of a second and similarly dressed Len. Len's 'good' ghost had given the correct response to the secret code. His 'evil' ghost continued to stare embarrassingly at Eddie, apparently unaware of, and blind to the new ghost.

"What are you looking at?" asked the evil ghost.

Eddie did not turn back or reply. With the good ghost already running back up the beach, Eddie quickly did likewise with the good Len shouting,

"Run, Eddie – as fast as you can, mate!"

Eddie didn't stop until they had both reached the pier, further down the promenade. Predictably, given their phantom guises, neither boy was out of breath. Eddie looked back, but the evil ghost had disappeared. Len was first to comment.

"Oh, Eddie! What have I told you? You must remember the code when we meet. I have a good side and an evil side and he was my bad ghost."

Eddie looked a little sheepish and embarrassed by his simple error.

"Sorry, mate; I just forgot."

"We'd better change the code again," said Len.

"What do you suggest?" asked Eddie.

"It can be anything – we'll just make something up now."

Eddie looked doubtful.

"Won't your evil ghost be listening? After all, he is part of you."

"Not now I'm dead, I think. I don't seem to have evil thoughts anymore. He's a totally separate entity."

"You think? You mean, you hope, comrade," said Eddie.

"Well, he didn't know about your mother's middle name, did he?"

"You heard him speak, then?" asked Eddie.

"Yes."

Eddie was clearly still not convinced because he then said,

"The evil ghost knew about our trip to Rome; the timings and my accident, you know. He was with you then."

Though Len went quiet, the news didn't seem to bother him too much.

"I told you he's a separate entity. I have no control over where he goes. We'll just have to hope that he's elsewhere right now. He didn't know the last code."

"I suppose you're right," said Eddie as he thought for a moment. His mathematical mind soon provided an idea for the code.

"What is the twentieth prime number, Len?"

Len looked totally bemused.

"You are joking, aren't you? How on earth would I know that?"

"It's seventy-one, mate."

"Seventy-one? I suppose that'll do – after all there's no way I would have been able to work that out while I was still alive!"

"True!" agreed Eddie and Len smiled back at his friend.

"You know it works both ways, don't you, Eddie?"

"What do you mean?"

"I mean that you have an evil side as well so that there's probably a bad 'Eddie' ghost wandering around out there."

Eddie looked a bit nervous for a moment until Len said,

"We'll just have to ask each other the question."

"No need, Len – as long as the correct question and answer are exchanged, it doesn't matter who asks it. Only we know the precise question and the answer."

Len looked knowingly at his friend.

"You're right again, maestro! You were always the genius at school."

"And you were the brilliant athlete and sportsman, Len. I feel safe again knowing you're with me again on equal terms, you know."

"We'll make a great team as ghosts, eh?" said Len.

Within ten minutes the boys found themselves, whether by design or not, in the High Street of Fenton-on-Sea on the busy Saturday morning at the end of July. Passing by or through the shoppers, Eddie began to sense a certain excitement in their faces and demeanour. Suddenly, as the two friends paused outside Woolworth's, Eddie understood the reason for the many smiling faces. A previous meeting with Len's ghost, almost at the moment of Len's tragic passing, had occurred in the future the day after this date – July the 30th, 1966. Len seemed to realise what Eddie was thinking.

"You know what today is, don't you?" he said.

"I think so," replied Eddie. "I remember this date from back in January – it's the World Cup Final this afternoon at Wembley."

"Spot on, and England are in it against West Germany."

Somewhere in the deep and dark recesses of Eddie's mind lurked something that was struggling to surface into a concrete fact, but nothing immediately presented itself to him. Strangely, he just felt he ought to know the score even before the game had been played. For his part, it was clear that Len did not possess such prior knowledge also.

"Hope we win," he said. "I think Germany are favourites, though."

Eddie suddenly felt exhausted; he remembered how easily his friend seemed to tire when he too had first taken on his ghostly role. He tried hard to fight the vagueness that threatened to take control of his new and delicate psyche. He had earlier been thinking about and looking forward to exploring his old haunts in his home town, not least of which was number 38 Fir Tree Close which he had left for the final time on a Saturday morning in late January earlier that year. He had a longing, of sorts, to see his family again; his sister, Jennifer – Jenny; his mother, Mrs Ann Compton and his father, Mr Fred Compton. Though he did not now possess the delicate and transitory emotions of a living and breathing person, he, nevertheless, thought it would be nice to see how his closest relations were doing. Jenny would be twenty now. Had she managed to keep her place at Hamsden Civic College on the hairdressing and beauty course? Was she still going out with Gary Jones? Was the relationship heading for permanence? All these thoughts rushed almost instantly through Eddie's ghostly mind. He seemed to have developed the ability to sift and process several different ideas simultaneously and even his friend's next few words hardly disturbed those thought patterns.

"You look tired, Captain," said Len, almost reading his friend's blank but slightly wistful face. Eddie emerged from his trance with a ghostly shudder, his brain and mouth appearing to work independently of his current thought process.

"Yeah, mate – almost enough excitement for one day."

"Pity," said Len. "I was going to suggest a trip down to London this afternoon; it's only about eleven now."

Eddie seemed to perk up.

"You mean you can take us to the game?"

"Why not? At least I can try to spirit us there. My ghostly powers have developed somewhat since we last met, and I managed to get us to Rome, didn't I?"

By now the two boys were 'resting' their ghostly forms against the glass frontage of Woolworth's window, unbeknown to the many passers-by. Eddie seemed to be drifting into sleep and invisibility, and within seconds he began to vanish from his best friend's ghostly view. Len whispered softly, though no one could now hear either of the two young ghosts,

"Come back, Eddie; stick with me – I need to be able to see you. You'll feel refreshed after our invisible journey. Please come back."

Eddie's ghostly form reappeared briefly and instantly Len began to contort his face while he concentrated on spiriting them through space and, maybe, time. Eddie saw and felt nothing apart from that now almost familiar warm glow inside him. His 'world' went dark as he drifted into oblivion. His initial awakening had lasted less than an hour.

2

Wembley

The next time Eddie came back to the land of the 'living dead', he felt somewhat refreshed and more relaxed than his first awakening into the bright sunshine of Fenton-on-Sea. Before his eyes began to open involuntarily, the first contact with his new world was via the medium of sound. A staccato chant pervaded Eddie's head.

"England! England! England!"

The next contact should have been physical had he been clothed in physical flesh. He would have found it hard to stand up as the crowds thronged and jostled along Wembley Way; a cacophony of sound emanating from a rolling ocean of red and white. For Eddie it was different. He seemed to be able to stand still without fear of being crushed by or pushed along on the crimson tide. He could, if he had wished, outrun the excited crowd and dodge, weave or just go straight through the unseeing bodies making their slow but relentless progress towards the twin towers. Where to go? That was the question.

"England! England!"

The chants were incessant. Eddie veered left as Wembley Way opened up into a large plaza before the stadium. He put himself into the largest open space he could find away from the eager and expectant crowds. All he could do was watch and wait. The clock high on the stadium read ten to three. The crowds began to thin out. Where was Len? Was he going to come and meet him or was it up to Eddie to find his friend? Five minutes passed. Eddie heard a roar from inside the stadium. The teams had obviously taken the field. No one came.

A loud whistle blew; the crowd observed a respectful silence; '*God Save the Queen*' rose to the heavens. Eddie walked nonchalantly to the nearest turnstile. No one challenged him as he glided smoothly into the ground.

The teams were lined up facing each other when Eddie at last found a suitable vantage point high up in the stand and almost opposite the half-way line. England were to attack the goal to Eddie's left. Len had still not put in an appearance. Had he been capable of human emotions, Eddie would have found the experience rather scary as he stood alone among the thousands of unknown fans. As it was, he felt relaxed and excited by the prospect of being able to watch the game, almost like a god, from his superb position above the field of play. Unlike all the other fans, Eddie found he could stand at the top of one of the wide gangways while stewards ushered the latecomers past, or occasionally, through him. He could also, if he wished, move freely around the ground and even venture onto the pitch if he could build up the confidence to do so. No one would see him, would they? He was a ghost after all. But did he have the faith to believe he would remain invisible and silent to everyone? Would God allow him to accomplish such an outrageous exploit? It would be a good way of making Len aware that he was in the ground. Surely he would then be spotted by his best friend from whatever position he himself had found? He would still be visible to Len, wouldn't he?

After a few minutes, the crowd were suddenly hushed. A ball crossed into England's penalty area was misheaded by the full back, Ray Wilson and Helmut Haller burst through to beat the diving Gordon Banks; 1–0 to West Germany. Only twelve minutes had passed. While the teams made their way back to the centre-circle, Eddie continued to look at his forlorn hero, Banksy, as he stood in the goalmouth in frustration at the ease with which the opposition had scored. Then Eddie saw him – standing nonchalantly leaning against the left-hand post, arms folded and shaking his head at the England goalkeeper. It had to be Len! Even at a hundred yards away, Eddie could make out his friend's distinctive blond hair and that bold, god-like pose. Eddie quickly made his decision and wandered silently and unnoticed down the gangway to the low retaining wall which he straddled with ease. Jumping onto the touchline and past the St John's Ambulance men, the linesman and some other important onlookers, Eddie headed for the right-hand goal, still not yet having the courage to walk directly across the pitch to his friend. Another German attack was imminent and Gordon Banks rushed into the centre of his penalty area. Eddie was now behind the goal and Len had moved away from the goalpost. Eddie whispered as loud as he dared,

"Len, I'm here, behind you!"

There was no response from his friend who was concentrating earnestly on the failed German attack as the ball now headed upfield and away from danger. Gordon Banks returned to his position on his goal line. Eddie crept closer, pretending to hold onto the goal netting for presumed security. He stood inches behind his friend and said quietly,

"I'm here, comrade."

Still no reaction. England had been awarded a free kick midway in the German half. Len seemed to tense. Eddie could hear Gordon Banks shout,

"*Go on, Bobby, swing it in for Geoff!*"

Bobby Moore lined up the kick. The crowd looked on excitedly. Eddie moved in front of Len, possibly blocking his view. Instantly Len moved to his right and shouted,

"Get out of the way, you idiot! I can't see!"

The free kick swung into the area. Geoff Hurst leapt unmarked and glanced his header beyond the astonished keeper; England had equalised and the crowd erupted in a sea of red and white. Len jumped high in the air and then spun round to face his friend.

"You made it, then, Captain."

"Yes, and you knew I was behind you, didn't you?" replied a slightly cross Eddie.

"Just my bit of fun, Eddie – I actually saw you outside in Wembley Way and followed you into the ground. We must have landed outside within feet of each other. Once inside I kept my eye on you until the game started and then I made my way here. I knew you would eventually see me if I stood by the goal, but I didn't expect them to score so easily or so early. Wilson made a real howler with his header to let that blond-haired bloke score."

Len paused and looked quizzically at his friend and when there was no immediate response to his facial promptings, he said,

"Well, what have you got to tell me, old son?"

"Not much – my arrival here was pretty much as you described."

Len grinned wryly. The game had restarted and the play had shifted back to the German penalty area. Len persevered with his questioning.

"And you're sure there's nothing else you want to *ask* me?"

And then Eddie realised his mistake and his ghostly face reddened to match his ginger hair.

"Whoops, Len! I'm sorry, mate."

"No need to say sorry to me, Eddie. Anyone could make such a *prime* mistake."

"So what is the twentieth prime, comrade?" asked the embarrassed Eddie.

"I believe that would be the number seventy-one, Captain, sir," replied Len.

The secret codes having been exchanged correctly, the two ghosts stood side by side to concentrate on the game as it entered a crucial stage.

"Next team to score wins it," said Len.

"Let's hope it's us, then," replied Eddie who was unaware that, in his embarrassment and excitement, he had encroached a few yards onto the pitch. Len quickly joined him as they both struggled to see the action in the distance at the other end. Eddie had almost read his friend's mind before Len eventually said,

"You know there's nothing to stop us just wandering right into the middle of the pitch and getting right up close to the players and the ball."

Eddie moved nervously back to the touchline. Len could not be serious, could he?

"No way, Len," he whispered from his new position of relative security, but as soon as he'd said it, he knew what Len would do. Despite his nervousness, Eddie also knew that they had been invisible and silent to everyone so far. If they did become visible they were, after all, just ghosts. They had no physical form. No one could catch them and who would believe anyone who said they'd seen a ghost in the middle of the pitch at Wembley! How ridiculous would that be? Eddie made a quick decision and followed his friend onto the pitch.

Back in April, Eddie's dad, Fred Compton, had reached a milestone in his working career with British Rail – he had, either side of the war, completed twenty-five years as ticket collector, guard and finally, senior clerk in the booking office at Fenton-on-Sea railway station. The management and his colleagues had bought him and his wife, Ann, a couple of special gifts, one permanent and one to be used on Saturday, July the 30th that year. Because of the tragedy that the respected couple had suffered in January, the gifts were rather more extravagant than was normal for such an occasion. Losing a son and not being able to bury him was more than most people could bear but Fred and Ann had been stoical in their grief and recovery, helped in no small way by the knowledge that their son had joined his best friend, Leonard Wilby, for an eternity of boyish fun and adventures.

The first gift was a beautiful silver pocket watch, appropriately inscribed and perfect for a man who had always been fastidious with his information on the timings of trains and in the day to day running of his private life, too. The second was to be shared with his wife or anyone else that Fred should choose to accompany him – two front row tickets for the World Cup Final at Wembley on the last Saturday in July. With England on home soil and one of the likely favourites, Fred had hoped all spring and early summer that Ramsey's boys would make it to the pinnacle of footballing success and reach the final. His prayers had been answered as he and Ann took up their seats just feet from the touchline and almost on half-way, giving them a perfect close-up view of the players and the game.

It was just a few minutes before half-time and the score still remained 1–1. Ann Compton was fidgety and in need of some natural relief, judging by some of the strange and awkward poses she was displaying in her seat.

"What is the matter, dear?" asked Fred, even though he knew the weakness of his wife's bladder.

"I need a wee," she whispered. "I'll have to go now, Fred."

"Can you go on your own? I don't want to miss any of the match."

"I think so. We passed some signs at the top of our gangway – you know I always keep a lookout when we go anywhere new."

"Don't be long, then. I'll look after your seat."

With her husband's blessing, Eddie's mum made her way quickly to the top of the stand. There were less than five minutes left before half-time. England were on the attack, but it was quickly broken up by a tall, young and handsome German player who in later years would become to be known as 'The Kaiser' and a thorn in England's side in many future games between the two countries; not only as a player either.

Meanwhile, Eddie and Len had 'ghosted' their ways past several England defenders, each of the phantom boys possessing a slippery and stealthy movement that not even the great Martin Peters would ever be able to emulate. They took up their positions in the middle of the centre-circle, from where they had just about the best view of anyone; player, referee or crowd alike. While Eddie remained more or less in a static position with his ghostly mouth wide open in sheer astonishment at their audacity and good fortune, Len did his best impression of a little dog as he pursued the ball everywhere round the pitch, even once standing inches in front of a German free-kick and pulling all kinds of faces at the player about to take it. He didn't even flinch when the ball seemed to shoot straight through his stomach and chest area without deflection or loss of speed. After a couple of minutes, Eddie began to relax when he eventually became absolutely certain that neither of them could be seen or heard by anyone. He ventured towards the touchline on the half-way line to watch an England throw-in to be taken by the captain Bobby Moore. Len joined him and began shouting at his blond hero,

""Throw it to Bally, Bob!"

As if by magic – although Len would swear later that it was *his* instruction that had penetrated Bobby Moore's mind – the ball was thrown directly to little Alan Ball who waltzed round two German players and set off for the opposition penalty area. Eddie stayed on the touchline while his friend skipped alongside the England number seven until Ball took on one too many defenders and the ball was cleared back up into the England half. Just before Eddie was about to set off to rejoin his fellow ghost back in the centre-circle, he suddenly heard a voice inside his head.

"*Turn round, Eddie; your dad's come to see you.*"

The words had hardly registered with Eddie before his body seemed to turn round of its own accord to face the crowd. He immediately got the shock of his life (?). There, not ten feet away in the front row, sat his dad. Eddie moved right to the retaining wall and in an almost nonchalant voice, said quietly,

"Hello, Dad. How have you been?"

No sooner had the words left his lips than Eddie realised how stupid he'd been in expecting to get an answer – ghosts couldn't be heard by ordinary people! He smiled to himself as he walked away, thinking how lucky his dad had been to get a ticket for the final. Once back on the pitch, Eddie turned back once more and gave a cheery wave to his dad. He hadn't felt much emotion at the strange meeting. He hadn't really felt much of anything. He was reminded of Len's words, when he had been alive, about ghosts not having the same feelings as living people. It seemed true – he felt neither happy nor sad at having seen his dad once again. It was just another event to be catalogued in his new life/death. However, he was reassured that his dad had looked well and happy which seemed to please him, but where was his mum? Was she still at home or had she come with his dad? Eddie rejoined his friend just as the referee blew his whistle for half-time and Len motioned to Eddie that they should follow the England team to their dressing room. At first Eddie looked reluctant, but as soon as Len began to disappear from the pitch he quickly followed suit, not wishing to be left alone on the pitch surrounded by one hundred thousand real living people!

Fred Compton was still rubbing his eyes in disbelief and muttering to himself.

"It couldn't have been him; it just couldn't have been. Eddie's dead – dead and gone."

"What did you say, dear?"

Ann Compton had returned carrying two ice-cream cornets.

"Wha …? Oh, nothing, love. I thought I saw someone I knew in the crowd," he lied.

"Who?"

"Oh nobody you would know. Just someone from work."

Fred's wife looked at him oddly. She was fairly certain that no one else from Fenton station had got tickets for the final. She sat down beside her husband and handed him his ice-cream which he promptly dropped onto the ground, his hands shaking uncontrollably. Ann Compton knew immediately that something was wrong. Her husband was clumsy at times but he would never drop an ice-cream. Never!

"Whatever is the matter, dear? You look like you've seen a ghost."

And then Fred Compton knew he would have to tell his wife. He began to stammer.

"I know you won't believe me but I-I think I've seen Eddie."

Ann Compton went silent and her face went deathly white. The two of them had hardly spoken about their departed son after the first few days of mental anguish. Because no body had ever been found, both of them, in their own ways, still harboured hopes that he would be found alive, even after over six months. Fred's wife, however, was made of sterner stuff and quickly gained her composure, dismissing any impossible thoughts back to the deep recesses of her mind where they belonged. She and Fred had to continue with their lives and not dwell in the imaginings of the past.

"Oh don't be daft, Fred. You know he's gone. Was it just another of your visions? I still see Eddie in my mind, you know, but that's all it is – just in my mind."

Ann tried to bring her husband back to reality by licking her ice-cream tantalisingly in front on his face. Fred seemed to brighten up a little.

"I don't know dear. I just can't believe what I saw. He was standing right in front of me, just by the wall and, Ann ...."

"What?" gurgled Ann Compton through her ice-cream.

"He was on the pitch, right by Bobby Moore and he came over and said hello to me."

"Oh now you're talking absolute nonsense, love. No one else could have seen him or else there would have been a real commotion. Shall I ask that chap next to you if he saw a strange boy walking on the pitch? I will if you like."

"No, of course not. I suppose you're right – it *was* all in my mind. Perhaps I just wanted to see him on today of all days. You know how much he would have loved to have been here to watch the final."

"I know, dear and he is in spirit, I'm sure. Now, shall I go and get you another ice-cream?"

"No, I'm alright now – just my mind playing tricks on me. I mean, how could a fourteen-year-old boy get onto the pitch unnoticed?"

"Precisely," said Ann Compton.

Fred sat back in his seat and tried to relax while he waited for the players to return for the second-half. Despite the couple's agreed explanation for what he thought he had seen, Fred Compton would remain convinced of what he had actually seen and heard for some time to come. One thing prevented him from pursuing the matter further and possibly with the authorities too. After his son had turned and waved to him from the pitch, Eddie had vanished into thin air, spirited away in as

26

quick a flash as he had appeared. Fred Compton was fairly certain that he had had an encounter with his son's ghost. The question that was nagging him, while he stared blankly at the empty pitch, was: 'Would he have more encounters with his son?' In some strange way, Fred Compton rather hoped he would.

The England dressing room was steamy as tired bodies exuded moisture after forty-five minutes of toil; shirts were soaking wet both from sweat and the effects of a couple of unseasonable rain showers. Thunder had been heard in the distance but the dressing room was oddly quiet as Alf Ramsey stood, besuited like a bank manager, and talked without emotion about what he wanted his players to do in the second-half. It really was like he was merely telling his team that they only had to do such and such and they would win. His ordered and unflappable approach seemed to breathe confidence into the players beyond that which their abilities warranted. Eddie and Len sat side by side at one end of the changing room and watched in awe as the great man explained carefully his tactics for the second-half. A simple '*Now go and win it*' echoed in the eleven gladiator's ears as they eventually strode back onto the turf at the end of the interval. The two boys followed them out in silence realising they had witnessed a master at work. All the team had to do, led by the colossus that was Bobby Moore, was follow the maestro's instructions as spelt out and in another forty-five minutes England would be World Champions.

Neither boy had said anything to each other while they had been sat in the dressing room; they had been too much in awe of the close proximity of all the fabulous footballers who, up until that day, had been nothing more than names that they had read about or seen occasionally on television. In the pause while the players lined up again for the second-half, Eddie told Len about seeing his dad in the stands. Len seemed more interested in the event than Eddie thought he would have been, given the fact that his own dad had died with him in the tragic car crash. As they stood in the centre-circle waiting for the referee's whistle, Len said,

"Show me where you saw him, mate."

Ignoring the play that had started, Eddie led his friend to the far touchline where his dad had been sitting. Len became quite excited when they found Eddie's mum and dad sitting next to each other and, like Eddie earlier, shouted a greeting from the touchline. Eddie hung back a little and even though he didn't show it, he did feel some comfort at seeing his mother again. Both his parents seemed well and happy, judging by their smiling faces and linked arms. It had pleased Eddie to see them, albeit in an unemotional sort of way, like a box that had been ticked in his progress as a ghost. He called to Len,

"Come on, mate; they can't see or hear you. Let's get on with the game – I don't want to miss a goal."

Len turned away from Eddie's parents; he too seemed able to quickly put his unusual meeting behind him and he ran past his friend and into the opposition half where another England free-kick was about to be taken by Captain Moore. This time, Len appeared to sit on the ball while Moore lifted it into the penalty area causing Len to jump into the air in a show of mock pain and surprise. Eddie arrived at his friend's side just as Len was making more drama over climbing painfully to his feet. Out of the corner of his eye, Eddie saw Roger Hunt head Bobby Moore's free-kick narrowly wide. The stadium clock read ten past four and in their seats, Eddie's parents were once again enjoying the match, both unaware of their son's best friend's attempt to make contact – they had neither seen nor heard anything untoward.

After a while, Eddie and Len began to get a little bored with chasing the ball and pulling faces at the German players, or the referee, occasionally shouting comments at both parties in an attempt to sway the progress of the game, but, of course, to no avail – as ghosts their powers did not yet extend to the miraculous. They were being allowed to keep just a watching brief. The match was nearly entering the last ten minutes when England were awarded a corner. While Eddie remained by the centre-circle, Len trotted forward and turned to shout to him from his advanced position on the edge of the German penalty area,

"I hope Bally takes it and swings it in for big Geoff!"

From his own position nearly thirty yards away, Eddie couldn't hear his friend's pointless remark, but Alan Ball duly obliged as requested and Geoff Hurst seemed to complete Len's pleading only for the big number ten's shot to be deflected. Fortunately it rebounded to England's footballing ghost, Martin Peters, who strode forward and slotted the ball home. The crowd, who had been quiet for some time, erupted in a deafening crescendo. Len turned to his fellow ghost and smiled with a look of, '*I told you so*!' Eddie merely punched his fist in the air and shouted,

"Two – one! Two – one! Come on the boys in red!"

The two boys followed the England players back to the centre-circle for the restart; there were just over ten minutes left. Surely England could hold on and they almost did until, in the very last minute, the Germans were awarded a free-kick a few yards outside the penalty area on the left-hand side of the field. Lothar Emmerich, the opposition number eleven and winger was delegated to take it. It had been given for a highly innocuous, albeit slightly clumsy challenge, by the tall and gangly Jack Charlton; Len had understandably shouted to the referee,

"That was never a foul, ref – the clown just fell over! Big Jack never touched him!"

The boys watched nervously from the edge of the area as the young German forward swung the ball in low and menacingly. Full-back George Cohen could do nothing more the block the kick as he attempted to clear it, but the ball skewed to Wolfgang Weber who rushed through to score. Gordon Banks ran to the referee patting one of his palms to indicate that there had been a handball by one of the Germans as the ball had crossed into the six-yard box, but the referee waved him away and the goal stood. Karl-Heinz Schnellinger, the likely handball culprit, made his way back to his own half, hiding his guilt brilliantly. The boys stalked him on his nonchalant walk, Len even trying to trip him up in his frustration and disappointment. On the way back to the centre-circle, Len mumbled to Eddie,

"That should never have been allowed. It wasn't a foul in the first place and then that bloke handled it. That Swiss referee needs to see an optician."

"He might need to see a doctor after the game, if he gets out of the ground alive," said Eddie with equal annoyance at the obvious injustice.

The game restarted, but in no time at all, the referee blew the whistle for full-time and the England players trudged to the touchline to join their manager for a pep talk before the statutory period of extra time. The Germans were smiling and those of them that were not totally exhausted had a spring in their step after their 'lucky' escape. Len and Eddie stood audaciously right next to Alf Ramsey, one on each side of him, nodding sagely to the players at every word he uttered. The 'bank manager' was again calm and collected; no panic, or even frustration, seemed to be etched on his face. No shouting, no histrionics, just a calm delivery of his message that they, the players, would have to go and win the game all over again. He told them that they were the better side and deserved to win, so that's all there was to it. He then left the players to their own thoughts and preparation with just one final word to his rock, Bobby Moore, who nodded his agreement to whatever instruction had been given. Meanwhile, the German manager, Helmut Schön, was talking non-stop with an animated expression on his face while the German players seemed to be far away in worlds of their own. The England team had listened to their manager in silence and with as much concentration as their tired bodies would allow in the circumstances. Time would tell as to which had been the more effective team talk.

The first ten minutes of added time were a tense and careful affair with neither side being too adventurous. With only a few minutes left of the first period, the ever-industrious Alan Ball put in a cross for Geoff Hurst to turn, swivel and shoot from close range. The ball hit the underside of the bar with both boys having taken up positions next to the England number ten. They watched excitedly as the ball dropped, almost in slow motion to the ground, both of them willing the ball to fall down behind the goal line. Len even shouted the hoped-for result while the ball was still feet off the ground.

"Goal! It's a goal – we've scored!"

Geoff Hurst turned to the Swiss referee with arm aloft, claiming the goal. German heads shook in denial. Referee Mr Dienst looked uncertain. Ninety thousand of the crowd bayed,

"Goal! Goal!"

To the right, the linesman had his flag raised. What did it mean? Eddie and Len ran over to him quicker than any of the players and almost before Mr Dienst had spotted him. Eddie was shouting,

"It wasn't off-side, mate. The ball was over the line!" and then he added inanely, "I saw it; I was only feet away. It was a goal."

Mr Dienst trotted over and Swiss/Russian sign language ensued. Mr Bakhramov nodded vehemently. German players wagged fingers and shook their heads. Mr Dienst made his decision, correct or not and, as if to make sure that there would be no argument, the linesman seemed to agree and pointed his flag to the centre-circle. Had Mr Bakharov been trying to signal off-side, but had 'chickened out' at the last moment? A jury vote of nine to one might have been a powerful catalyst in the final decision. This time, it would be Eddie that would say later that his own shouting and gesticulation in front of the linesman had persuaded him to award the goal. Whatever the real reason, which would perplex fans and pundits alike for years, the goal stood; England led 3–2 and Eddie and Len trotted merrily back to the centre, heaping their praises on big Geoff Hurst as they ran beside him.

The rest of the first period and most of the second continued to be a tense affair with neither side giving an inch. Alf Ramsey had been once again calm and confident at the interval, saying very little except the odd quiet word to one or two players. As far as he was concerned, England were justly in front and would go on to win the game.

The last minute beckoned and a reckless German attack broke down. Many of their defenders had gone forward in a desperate attempt to score a last-minute goal. Booby Moore spotted the defensive gaps and kicked the ball deep downfield to the unmarked Geoff Hurst who raced forward and blasted an unstoppable shot into the top left-hand corner of the net. Some people had run onto the pitch to join the two boy-ghosts in premature celebrations. The score was 4–2 and England were going to win the World Cup. Though commentator Kenneth Wolstenholme's words, 'Some people are on the pitch. They think it's all over …,' would become a fitting epitaph for the nation's victory for years to come, their true meaning would only ever be fully understood by two beings who had actually preceded the pitch invasion by nearly two hours. If either of the two boys had managed to hear the famous words, they would have both laughed inwardly at all the fuss and attention concentrated on the few living souls who had dared to run onto the pitch during play. It had almost been commonplace for the two ghostly teenagers!

3
Visitations

A few seconds after the referee blew his whistle for the end of extra time, and therefore of the whole match, Eddie's presence on Wembley's hallowed turf ended abruptly with a return to blackness and oblivion. His second awakening had lasted less than three hours. He would sadly miss his friend's antics as Bobby Moore lifted the Jules Rimet trophy high above his head; the grinning Leonard Wilby doing a 'Nobby Stiles' type jig at his side. He also would miss seeing Len trying to 'fly' from the presentation balcony as a quick way of getting back to the pitch. If the daring young ghost had been a living and breathing person, he would have surely ended up with several broken bones or worse. As it was, his aerial trick was cut short when he too returned to the sleeping state of oblivion. As would become the norm on such occasions, the two ghosts would not necessarily depart their earthly visitations at the same time. Unlike in life, they really had become 'free spirits' although under strict but random control from on high. God was their master now and he would determine when they next met. Until that time they would 'sleep' without form or any kind of restriction on time. Len had been accustomed for some time to being on his own when making earthly visits; Eddie had not. He still had much to learn on his new journey.

Ann and Fred Compton managed to get back to their ember-red and cream Hillman Minx by half past six, a remarkable achievement given the huge and excited crowd that left Wembley that afternoon. Fred had decided to park a good half a mile away from the ground. He was pleased to see his car had survived its visit to the huge open car park unscathed;

no scratches or bumps that he could see. Within fifteen minutes they were back on the A406 North Circular Road and heading for the A12 that would eventually take them back to Hamsden and thence by the A132 the final twelve miles to their East Anglian seaside home in Fenton-on-Sea. Fred Compton still seemed rather tense on the return journey. Ann did not question him and remained quiet until he had negotiated the unfamiliar roads back beyond Romford. It was to her relief that, as soon as he spoke, she realised that the tenseness had been due to the unfamiliarity of the road system rather than any aftermath of what he had told her earlier that afternoon.

"*Now* I know where I am," he said. "I've been guessing for the last hour, you know."

"You must have had a guardian angel guiding you, love," replied his wife with a knowing smile.

"What – you mean Eddie?"

"Well, you never know. I often think he's watching us."

They were on the A12 now and Fred flicked the switch to turn the lights on. It was well over a month past mid-summer and with the cloudy evening, at eight o'clock it was starting to get dark. Ann Compton sat back in her seat and her eyes began to feel heavy as she drifted off to sleep, aided by the Hillman's encouraging engine noise. For the first time for a while that day, Fred began to relax also and, with his wife asleep, he thought about the earlier visitation from his son. He remained convinced that he had seen Eddie's ghost that afternoon and that his son had seen him in return. His wife's words suddenly came back to him: '*I often think he's watching us*'. He steeled himself to look in his rear-view mirror, but when he did he saw only the reflection of dull headlights and grey/black tarmac. '*Don't be daft, Fred*', he told himself. A cold shudder went up his spine and he focused his mind and eyes on the road ahead, trying to read

35

the number plates of the cars in front of him and the mileposts as they flashed by: '*Colchester 12, Hamsden 31*'.

The Comptons made it safely home to 38 Fir Tree Close that evening, without alarms or delays. Ann Compton didn't wake up until they had already passed Linham a few miles from journey's end. The next few weeks remained uneventful for them both as the school holidays passed into September. It had been a busy time for Fred in the station booking office; the weather had been good for travelling by rail and the whole country was still bathing in the excitement of England's victory in the World Cup. People were relaxed and enjoying the warm weather by taking days out; the train suited many for the comfort and worry-free journeys it provided.

September moved into October and Fred's duties became easier as passengers were mainly restricted to commuters and local people bound for Hamsden's reasonable shopping centre. Thus it was that Fred had had a quiet morning on Wednesday, October the 19th and by ten o'clock, the station was more or less empty of passengers needing guidance or tickets. Taking the opportunity afforded by the lull in business, Fred made his way to the back of the booking office to do some general tidying up and filing. He hadn't left the front counter for much more than a minute when the push-bell sounded. It rang twice more before he returned to the glass window. This customer was clearly impatient for a ticket or, possibly, just directions. Fred was almost speechless when he heard the client's question.

"I need a ticket to Ludmouth in Devon, please."

The stranger was a man of about six feet with greying swept-back hair and a pleasant smile. His accent, though faint, wasn't local and Fred was pretty certain that he hadn't seen the well-dressed man before. But there was something about his manner and his speech that seemed familiar to Fred Compton. Apart from his own family holidays taken by rail to the south Devon seaside town in a couple of previous summers, no one had ever requested a ticket to the quiet Devon backwater. On both of the family holidays, Eddie's friend, Leonard Wilby, had accompanied them with almost fatal consequences when, on the second occasion, the two boys, having wandered onto a disused railway line, had nearly been run down by a shunting engine. Many memories flashed through Fred Compton's head as he tried to regain his composure to reply to the stranger's unusual request.

"Will that be a single or a return, sir?"

"Oh, a single will do."

"Do you know the route, sir?" asked Fred politely and with more confidence.

"I think so – Hamsden, Liverpool Street and then a train west from Waterloo. Am I right?"

Fred looked a little surprised at the stranger's knowledge.

"Yes, that's correct, sir. Just remember to change at Exeter."

"Of course, and I guess the train from there only goes to Ludmouth Junction, right?"

"Yes, sir," said Fred.

"How much will that be, please?"

Fred made great play of looking through timetables and price lists, even though he knew the fare off by heart.

"That's four pounds, seventeen shillings and sixpence, sir," he said eventually. "The next Hamsden train is at twenty to eleven."

The stranger nodded politely and placed what looked like a brand new five-pound note in the revolving tray and said,

"Thanks, Fred – keep the change."

With that, he picked up the ticket, Fred having already turned the tray so that it was on the customer side. The man then turned to walk away, leaving Fred with astonishment written all over his face. After a few paces, the man turned back and over his shoulder, said,

"Eddie's doing fine, Mr Compton – he's happy now. Remember me to your lovely wife. Tell her that George sends his regards."

Fred Compton's eyes seemed to glaze over and thus he hardly noticed that the strange man had vanished instantly from view. Almost on auto-pilot and certainly by force of habit, Fred turned the revolving tray round and his nightmare suddenly got worse. The tray was completely empty! He was torn between two possible courses of action. One: go after the man or, two: try and find the missing five-pound note. He went for the former and ran out of his booth, his mind racing and his heart pumping, but it didn't take him more than a few minutes to search Fenton's small and compact railway station. The man was nowhere to be seen. Fortunately, no one else had turned up at the ticket office when he returned, breathless and shaking with fear. The crisp new note was nowhere to be seen either; it hadn't slipped out of the tray and onto the floor, and there had been nobody else in the vicinity who might have picked it up. Eventually, Fred found himself slumping into his old leather armchair at the back of the office. He had put a sign in the booth window: 'Back in ten minutes'. He needed time to think.

The voice, and then the words that the man had spoken, had confirmed the identity of the strange man in Fred's mind. George Canter had been, up until about three years previously, owner of the junk shop in Mill Road. He had gone back to his native Poland after much criticism of, and doubts about, his selling methods for which, thankfully, he made amends before he left. But Fred had since learnt that Mr George Canter, or Georgi Kantechuk, to give him his birth name, had died of liver disease in his home town of Bialystok in eastern Poland. Fred knew what it meant – he had just had his second encounter with a ghost, but a much older version of the Polish Jew. The man's comment regarding his wife had merely served to rubber-stamp his conclusions – Fred had suspected that George Canter had been 'sweet' on her while he had lived in Fenton, even giving Fred cause to speak to him about it and to warn him off. Fred also remembered how George had taken an interest in his son, Eddie; although the incident with the mysterious object, which Eddie had purchased in Mr Canter's junk shop, had made Fred doubt the sincerity of that interest. The missing fiver fitted with Fred's ghostly conclusion also. But where was the ticket? A vanishing ghost who had no physical form couldn't take a small but solid object away, could he? Fred leapt up and rushed out to the forecourt in front of the ticket booth. A middle-aged lady was approaching. She came right up to Fred and said,

"I found this over by platform one. I think somebody must have dropped it and it's still valid for today."

Fred took the ticket and said robotically,

"Thank you, madam. I'll keep it until someone comes to claim it. I think I know who bought it. What a careless thing to do."

The lady made her way back to catch the Hamsden train which had just pulled into platform one. Fred Compton returned to his booth. Strangely, he felt better about the whole incident. It tied up a loose end over the ghostly meeting – the five-pound note hadn't been real but the ticket had, and ghosts couldn't take real things away. It made sense to Fred. Reality and fantasy (?) had just collided on Fenton-on-Sea railway station and Fred Compton had survived the extraordinary encounter. By the time his next customer arrived at the ticket office, his fear and uncertainty had been replaced by an inner calm when he recalled the ghost's words:

"Eddie's doing fine – he's happy now."

In some strange way, Fred Compton had just started a journey like his son before him. He would not be so afraid nor off guard if another such visitation should take place in the future. In the meantime, he thought it wise to keep his own counsel over the matter; his wife needn't be told – it would only cause her grief, or worse, if she formed the opinion that her son was still alive.

Gary Jones had been dating Eddie's sister, Jenny Compton, for well over three years and, though there had been some problems at the beginning of the relationship, the path of true love had been level and even for quite some time. Gary was twenty-two and, after spending three years of his life in various temporary jobs, including working rather reluctantly for his father at Richard Jones' Cars in Hamsden, he had, at nineteen, found a worthwhile career. He had recently completed his two-year probationary training programme in the fire brigade and had become a fully retained-firefighter. Jenny was in her second of two years at Hamsden Civic College. A month following her father's strange encounter with Mr Canter, the young couple were to be found taking coffee in the Steep Hill Tearooms overlooking the promenade gardens at Fenton-on-Sea. It was just after eleven on the morning of Saturday, November the 19th. Jenny was trying to discuss a matter that seemed to be making her boyfriend a little nervous and awkward.

"Well are we going to get married, then?"

Gary attempted a 'dead-bat' reply.

"We're far too young to think about things like that, Jen. I've only just started with the fire service proper a couple of weeks ago. We don't have any money saved yet and, anyway, where would we live?"

Jenny frowned at her boyfriend's dismissive answer and said,

"Getting married isn't just any *thing like that*. It's the most important thing that most people do in their lives, Gary, and besides …"

Gary was silent – he knew what was coming. Jenny was predictable when she continued.

"And besides, your parents are loaded. Surely they would help us out. You're mum idolises you since you became a fireman and got away from your dad."

Gary sighed and took a sip of coffee. Best let Jenny run out of steam before he replied. She poured on the heat.

"Don't you want to marry me, Gary? Don't you want to be with me every day *and* every night? Don't you want to have …?"

Gary couldn't remain silent any longer.

"Of course I do, love. It's not that and I suppose it's not the money either. It's just that …"

"Just what? If you love me and the money isn't an issue, what else is there?"

Gary looked embarrassed and said,

"I just don't feel ready for such an important step in my life. It's a huge responsibility to have a wife to look after and children to raise. It will tie us down for years. Now I'm earning some good money in a stable job, I want us to have some fun out of life. God knows you deserve it after losing your brother, and besides, you don't finish college until next summer. Then you'll have to get a job."

"Will I, Gary? queried Jenny coyly. "Can't I just be a lady of leisure and stay at home with my three children?"

"Now you're being silly," said Gary. "If we're to buy a house, we'll both need to work for a few years – you're still only twenty, Jen love."

Gary's cautious logic began to have the effect he'd planned. Jenny pouted and replied,

"Oh, I know you're right, Gary. You always are and that's why ..."

"That's why?" said Gary raising his eyebrows.

"That's why I L-O-V-E you," said Jenny spelling out every letter so that no one else in the tearoom should hear. As Gary leant across the table to kiss her, she glimpsed an old man at the adjoining table smiling at the young couple's public intimacy. Jenny looked slightly embarrassed before the young fireman sat back in his chair and said,

"I'll make you a promise, Jenny. I promise you that if you get a job next July when you finish college, then I'll marry you before the autumn of the following year. That should give us two years to plan the wedding and to save for the deposit on a house and so on. Deal?"

Jenny stuck out her bottom lip in a feigned sulk and replied,

"I suppose that will have to do, but aren't you forgetting something, Gary?"

Gary thought for a moment.

"No, I don't think so. Getting you a job, the wedding and buying a house are the only things we need to worry about."

Jenny pouted even more pointedly. How slow could her boyfriend be? She gave up her promptings and came straight to the point.

"I haven't said I'll marry you yet, you know."

Gary smiled.

"But you will, won't you."

"I might if you actually ask me, Gary!"

Gary looked really embarrassed now and after a brief pause while he scanned the tearoom to see if anyone was listening to their intimate conversation, he said quietly,

"Will you, Miss Jennifer Compton, at some time in the not too distant future, give me the greatest pleasure any man could ever have and do me the honour of becoming my wife?"

Jenny's mouth dropped in awe at Gary's beautiful and thoughtful words. She would realise later that Gary had probably been preparing himself for some time for such a moment as that grey November day. She was quick with her reply.

"Yes, Gary, I will."

Further kisses were exchanged and Jenny broke the tension with,

"Now go and buy me the most expensive engagement ring you can find."

In her highly charged emotional state, Jennifer Compton hadn't noticed that the old man had moved his chair much closer to their table and had probably heard much of what the two of them had said to each other. When he spoke, however, his words indicated a greater knowledge of Jenny's personal life than the couple's conversation might have suggested. He leant across and whispered in Jenny's ear. She instinctively lowered her head and looked down at the table.

"It's a pity that Eddie won't be present to see you get married, Jennifer. He still loves you, you know and you will see him soon, I have no doubt. Remember, you still share a secret."

Jenny froze and lifted her head to look at her boyfriend who seemed to be concentrating on the view out of the window to his side.

"Gary!" she started, but sensing movement at her side, she glanced in the old man's direction. She couldn't believe her eyes. In the brief second it had taken her to lift her head, look at Gary and then turn back to the old man, he had vanished.

"What, love? Whatever's up? You look like you've just seen a ghost."

To begin with, Jenny said nothing. It was clear from Gary's reaction that he hadn't seen the old man whisper to her. She tried to remain calm and find out what he had seen.

"I hope that old man didn't hear us talking, Gary."

"What old man?"

"The one who was sitting there at the next table."

Gary pulled an odd face at his girlfriend.

"No one's been sitting there all the time we've been here. That's why I chose this table. Those things I said were meant for your ears and your ears only, my love."

4

Eddie Awakes Alone

Jenny didn't immediately pursue her somewhat strange remark with her boyfriend and Gary, himself, didn't put it down to anything more than her nervousness caused by the emotion of the occasion. He was, however, concerned for her welfare and state of mind.

"Are you sure you're alright?"

Jenny pushed back her hair and tried to pretend that nothing untoward had happened.

"Must have been imagining things, I suppose."

Gary relaxed and, continuing to try to reassure Jenny, said,

"There was an old man in the tearooms earlier but he sat over there by the door. Maybe you caught a glimpse of him out of your eye and because of your excitement you thought he was a lot closer."

Jenny looked thoughtful. Was Gary just making it up to appease her or had there really been a man by the door? Jenny decided to seek confirmation one way or the other; she was careful with her choice of words.

"Oh him – you mean the really ancient old boy with long flowing white hair?"

"Yes, he looked like a biblical prophet; probably in his eighties."

So that was it, thought Jenny and she began to relax inwardly. Gary had described perfectly the man who had spoken to her. But she also knew that she was convinced that he had been sitting right by them on the closest table for some time. Gary must have seen him if he was …. The thought remained hanging in Jenny's mind. It had been a while, indeed, not since her brother had been alive, but she realised that she had just had another ghostly visitation.

Jenny decided to 'put the matter to bed' and said finally,

"Well at least I'm not going mad, then. I expect you're absolutely right. I do remember catching sight of an old man when we first came in. He looked so unusual he must have made such an impression on me that he was in my mind's eye when you asked me the vital question."

Gary smiled pleasantly.

"He looked a nice old boy – almost from another age."

Gary looked at his watch.

"God look at the time. It's gone twelve and the train goes at twenty past. We're going to have to run if we're going to make the afternoon performance at the Embassy cinema in Hamsden – the film starts at one-fifteen."

Jenny busied herself checking her make-up in her hand mirror while Gary paid the bill at the counter. They joined each other at the door where Jenny asked,

"And what are we going to see?"

"It's called *Blow-Up*," replied Gary. "It's supposed to be good."

"What's it about?"

"No idea, love, but what else can we do on a miserably grey day like today."

They were walking up the High Street by now and Jenny replied,

"Well, if we were married we could go home and make ….."

Gary didn't allow his girlfriend to finish her suggestive remark.

"Jenny! Don't be naughty."

They eventually made the film with five minutes to spare, and Jenny's previous involvement with the slim dividing line between reality and illusion continued. Parts of the film were a perfect reminder to her of the illusory event earlier that morning in the tearooms at the top of Steep Hill.

In the weeks leading up to Christmas, Jenny often thought back to that cold, grey morning in mid-November. She tried to convince herself that nothing really had happened but without much success. Though its memory started to wane, particularly with the excitement of Christmas approaching, she couldn't find any other explanation than her original and inevitable ghostly conclusion. The old man's words were both strange and comforting. What had he said? At first she couldn't quite remember them exactly until she decided to write her best recollection down in her diary. One day in early December she wrote,

'Eddie loves you and is coming to see you soon. It's a shame he won't see you married. He still shares your secret.'

Without really knowing it, Jenny had recorded the old man's remarks correctly, albeit, not in the same order nor with precisely the same words. The first part excited her to think she might see her brother again and the second reminded her that they had both had ghostly experiences before while Eddie had still been alive. She, at least, had told no one else of such happenings. Those events had served to convince her that the old man in November had been a ghost.

Eddie couldn't feel cold or heat or any other physical sensation and when he next awoke, it was only the absence of leaves on the trees and a white frost on the ground that told him it was winter. As before, he found himself on the seafront at Fenton-on-Sea, though not this time in a sitting position. Clothes, of course, were irrelevant to his situation but at least he had some on. Remarkably, when he looked down at himself, he discovered he was appropriately dressed for a winter's day, sporting his old duffle coat over some clothes that seemed familiar to him. He wasn't aware that all of the clothes he was wearing had been given away or destroyed some time ago. As he walked to the foot of Steep Hill, he chuckled to himself at the simplicity of his new existence – he didn't even have to dress himself, let alone wash or perform other necessary and natural human functions. He felt no tiredness or lessening of his walking speed as he negotiated the aptly named incline up to the High Street. Len had not yet appeared and though Eddie kept glancing around in the hope of seeing him, he wasn't unduly bothered that he hadn't shown his face. It would be fun to try out his new abilities on his own and he quickly made the decision that there was only one place that he wanted to go to that morning, for morning it seemed to be by the position of the winter sun. The town was virtually deserted and Eddie immediately deduced that it was a Sunday which, with the bells of St Andrew's Church sounding a coherent tune, narrowed the actual time down to just before eleven as the morning congregation was summoned to worship. Christmas decorations and gifts in the shop windows further narrowed the date to mid-December. Eddie's mental guess was pretty accurate given that it was actually Sunday, December the 18th, exactly one week before Christmas Day. The fact that it was still also 1966 was not yet apparent to Eddie as he reached South Road and the entrance to Fir Tree Close. Who would be at home at number 38? Should he have gone straight to St Andrew's where his parents were almost certain to be at that time on a Sunday morning? Would just his sister be at home? That would be quite nice, he thought as he glided up the front path of his old house, grinning to himself when he walked straight through the solid wooden front gate.

Jennifer Compton *was* at home that morning, but she wasn't well, having gone down with a bad cold at college on the Friday which, coupled with a nasty sore throat, had left her feeling very sorry for herself. This was made all the worse by the fact that her beloved Gary was on duty all weekend in Hamsden. She had taken up almost permanent residence in her bedroom that weekend, propped up by several pillows and surrounded by various pills, throat lozenges and tissues.

By eleven-thirty Jenny began to feel the effects of her second *Beecham's Powder* that morning and her eyes began to close as she gave in to a welcoming and healing sleep. Dreams came to her quickly, but nothing meaningful nor connected, just snippets of memories and emotions. Soon, however, they became more coherent and Gary began to figure in most of the random scenes, including several wedding visions, culminating inevitably in Jenny trying to form the words, '*I do,*' but without success. Her final dream became an impossible mixture of questions and strange interruptions. The important bit in church was not going to plan and Jenny was becoming distraught.

"*Will you take this man …?*"

"You lazy girl; always asleep."

"*… to have and to hold ….*"

"I come all this way and all you can do …."

"*… in sickness and in health ….*"

"For goodness sake, wake up!"

"*… as long as you both shall live ….*"

"Wake up, Jenny! Please wake up!"

If Eddie could have mustered up some kind of physical force, he would have sat on the bed and shaken his sister by the shoulders. He had to make do with his phantom urgings in the hope that they would permeate her sleep. He knew he wasn't making any human sounds or, at least, nothing that any living person could hear. Jenny began to stir and, with a moaning that seemed to say,

"Shut up and go away – I'm getting ma …," she woke with a start. Her head jerked backwards from its drooping position and glazed eyes stared into space from beneath her fevered and moist brow.

"Well, at last, Elizabeth Taylor awakes."

It was true that Jenny was awake at last but, as far as she was concerned, her dream was still continuing, for there, at the end of her bed, stood her recently departed brother, looking exactly the same as the last time she had seen him apart, that was, from his clothes – the clothes that she herself had helped get rid of.

"Eddie?"

As soon as she heard her own question she knew that she was finally awake and her dream was over. The old man had been right. Eddie had come to see her. She rubbed her eyes and looked again.

"I knew you'd come, Eddie. I just knew it," she said quietly.

Eddie's ghostly face seemed to frown.

"Oh yeah? How did you know? Even I had no idea I was coming here until about forty minutes ago."

"Someone told me I'd see you soon."

"Who? Someone I know?" asked Eddie, thinking that his best friend had been up to his tricks and had paid Jenny a visit without telling him.

"I don't know who he was, but I know he was a ghost. I saw him last month in the Steep Hill Tearooms when Gary and I had a coffee there."

"How did you know he was a ghost?"

"Because Gary didn't see him and yet the old man came and sat right beside me and whispered in my ear. Gary said there hadn't been anyone sitting next to us all the time we were there, so I just knew."

"Did you tell Gary you'd seen a ghost, then?"

"No – he wouldn't have believed me so what would have been the point?"

Jenny got up from the bed and moved to be beside her brother who was still standing at the foot of the bed. She tried to reach out and touch him and Eddie began to laugh.

"What *are* you doing? You can't feel me, you know."

Jenny gave a little squeal of surprise mixed with excitement as her hand passed through her brother's chest.

"Are you sure you can't feel that?" she asked.

"Of course not."

"Not even a tickle?"

"Jenny, I'm a ghost. Anyway what did this man look like? You said he was an old man."

Jenny returned to her bed where she curled her legs under her and continued to look in awe at her brother. *She* had questions to ask too.

"Yeah, really old – long flowing white hair and quite well-spoken with a posh voice and a bit effeminate – quite tall for an old man."

The description fitted only one man that Eddie had ever known and it confirmed his sister's story, for that man was indeed dead and able to walk a ghostly path. Aloyisious St John Grant had been the owner of Grants' Emporium for years before his untimely death in the Fenton train crash two years previously. Grant's Emporium had been turned into Steep Hill Tearooms after his death. How appropriate, thought Eddie, that the old man should put in an appearance in his old shop. Again, all these thoughts were processed much more quickly by Eddie's ghostly brain than any human one could have done and there was no apparent delay before Jenny asked,

"Do you know him, then? I mean, did you know him?"

Jenny seemed to be joining in quite naturally with the spirit of the conversation.

"I think so, and so did you. It sounds like it was Mr St John Grant, who used to own the Emporium on Steep Hill, where you and Gary ...."

"Where we had coffee?"

"Precisely."

"He died in the train crash, didn't he," said Jenny.

"Yes, he did."

Jenny started to fidget a little. She had many questions to ask her brother including the obvious one of how and when he had passed into his new 'state', but she also knew that her parents were due back at any time. Her bedroom alarm clock read twelve-thirty.

"Mum and Dad will be back soon, Eddie. You'll have to make yourself scarce."

Eddie did his best to laugh and Jenny realised at once that her statement had been a stupid one.

"I'll hang around and see them," said Eddie, "but, no, I won't make myself visible to them, Jenny."

"You mean you can disappear from view at will?"

"I hope so. I was invisible until I came into your bedroom. Beside, I thinking haunting people is an individual thing. No two people ever see the same things."

"You hope," said Jenny.

"Well if they do see me it will be a nice family reunion, eh?"

Jenny glanced at the clock. She knew she had to ask the question. She started nervously.

"Can I ask you a question, Eddie?"

"No need, I'm not going to give you an answer."

"You don't know what I'm going to ask."

"Don't be stupid, Jen, of course I do. You want to know what happened to me on that Saturday last January."

"Well?"

"I can't give you an answer, Jenny, because I don't know. All I can remember is catching the train to Hamsden and then my mind is a blank."

"Sally Barber said you told her you were going home when she and Liz Roberts met you at the station. Where did you go, Eddie?"

Eddie's ghostly face looked flustered and he feigned anger.

"I tell you, I just don't know – now change the subject."

Jenny went quiet for a few moments and Eddie turned to look out of the window. He couldn't tell his sister what had really happened that day – it would lead to all manner of discussions about his and Len's adventures over the previous three or four years. He couldn't recall the last and vital piece of the jigsaw anyway. He had been in Rome with Len's ghost, and then oblivion had subsumed him until he had returned as a ghost at the end of July. Though Jenny was sympathetic to and open-minded about the ghost world, she wasn't yet ready for his life story, oh no, not just yet! Just as he sensed that Jenny was about to ask another question, Eddie spotted his mum and dad coming up Fir Tree Close and the warm inner glow returned as he noticed them arm in arm, something that he had never seen them do when he had been alive. If he had had a working heart it would have been warmed with contentment. Instead, he turned back to Jenny and said,

"I'm awfully tired now, sis. I can feel myself going. It's been nice seeing you. I'll come again"

Eddie's image began to fade in front of Jenny and she just had time to say one last thing. She hoped it would register with her brother.

"Gary has asked me to marry him and I've said yes. We're getting married the year after next and …."

Eddie had all but vanished as Jenny finished in a rush of words.

… we're getting engaged at Christmas."

Eddie had gone. Jenny hoped that he had absorbed at least the first part of her final words. She curled up on her bed. She was so pleased that her brother seemed happy and that death appeared not to have the finality and terror that had always scared her from being a little girl, listening to all the doom and gloom about heaven and hell on a Sunday morning at St Andrew's Church. A minute or so later her mum poked her head round the door and said,

"How are you feeling, Jenny love? Not at death's door, are we?"

Jenny nearly replied that she actually had just been through it and had just got back but, instead, she said,

"No, Mum, but I am feeling a little better. Had a nice sleep with some pleasant dreams."

5

Some Harmless Fun

The 'Summer of Love' was in full swing when Eddie next broke the
shackles of death, and when he became aware of his surroundings, it was
obvious to him that he hadn't landed back in Fenton-on-Sea. His first
contact with the earthly world was through the medium of music.

> *'If you're going to San Francisco,*
> *be sure to wear some flowers in your hair ….'*

As he listened to the words of the song and while his eyes tried to
focus on the world around him, he thought initially that he had arrived in
the land of the free, but the accents of the people around him were
definitely Anglo-Saxon, even vaguely familiar – Len spoke with a similar
brogue. Finally, his ghostly eyes opened fully. He discovered he was
surrounded by a crowd of mostly young men and women, though with
their long flowing hair styles, it was difficult to tell the difference in some
cases, the final distinction often being the growth of facial hair on some
of the throng. Eddie noticed that some were carrying placards and,
straining his neck above the crowd, he could read some of the slogans.
'America out of Vietnam' and *'Ban the Bomb'* were among the
commonest. It was a mass protest of some kind and Eddie had found
himself right in the middle of it. As he kept pace with the massed crowds,
he tried to work out his location. Being still a fourteen-year-old boy who
was less than five feet in height made it difficult for him to see over the
people around him, tightly packed as they were as they rolled along. He
hadn't yet developed any ghostly skills which would have enabled him to
levitate above the crowd, and just passing through them seemed pointless
as the crowd stretched as far as a human eye could see in all directions.
The day was hot and, though Eddie had no feeling in that respect, he was

at least dressed for the occasion. Had he been visible – and who knows if he was – he would have drawn odd looks only because of his age and not because of his clothes which were an old summer shirt and jeans. The Almighty had got him ready for the day with suitable attire. A voice called to him from behind.

"You're a bit young for this, aren't you, sonny?"

Eddie stopped and turned round, allowing the crowd to pass by and through him. He stood still for a few seconds. The voice came again and from very nearby.

"Just keep walking, Captain; I'll catch you up in a minute."

And then Eddie knew who it was and within a few seconds Len was at his side, grinning like a Cheshire cat as he thrust his face into his own.

"Good morning, Eddie. Welcome to London."

So that was it, thought Eddie – a summer's day in England's capital and his best friend's birthplace. But he wasn't going to be caught out this time by the excitement of the situation. He had already been thinking of what he would and should say if Len had put in an appearance. Remaining in their standing positions while the last few stragglers of the crowd passed on, Eddie asked,

"Good morning to you too, comrade, and pray tell me, what is the twentieth prime number?"

For an awful moment Eddie thought Len was going to reply by questioning his sanity at receiving such a ridiculous request but he got the answer he had hoped for.

"Why that would be seventy-one, old sport. Am I right?"

"Spot on, Len. Good to see you."

The two boy-ghosts now found themselves virtually alone in a fairly large open space; alone apart from a few foreign tourists who clearly had no part in the receding demonstration. Eddie leant on his friend's superior knowledge of London.

"Where are we, mate?"

"Look over there," replied Len.

Eddie glanced up at the imposing sight of Nelson's Column.

"Well?" asked his friend and Eddie paused for thought.

"Erm – Trafalgar Square, I suppose."

"Well done, Captain."

They wandered over to a low stone wall where they sat down, or at least, pretended to. Their actual position in space and time had become less and less important to them but, just in case someone could see them, they took on normal human actions as best they could.

"What was that all about?" asked Eddie.

"Vietnam war protest, I think. Judging from what I could make out their all off to the American Embassy in Grosvenor Square."

"Did you also gauge what year we're in?" continued Eddie.

"Not sure really, but possibly 1967. It's definitely not 1966; there are no signs of World Cup fever. People's minds seem to be on other things."

"Hair styles have changed, Len. What's that all about? I thought Beatlemania was dead."

"They're called hippies, I think. They seem to protest against anything and everything," replied Len. "Especially anything to do with capitalism and America – hence the anti-Vietnam war demonstration."

Eddie smiled at his friend's trivialisation of life and anything controversial concerned with it. Len kept things simple. And, at that moment, his mind was on their more immediate prospects.

"So what do you fancy doing in the big metropolis?"

"Don't know. What is there to see?" asked Eddie.

Eddie had only once before been to London and that had been with Len too on a day-out by train from Fenton-on-Sea when they had both still been in the land of the living. On that occasion they had spent most of the day in the shopping areas of Oxford and Regent Street.

"London Zoo in Regent's Park is worth a visit and Covent Garden is good – they have lots of entertainment there. It's a bit pointless going shopping or looking for somewhere to eat, isn't it?"

"We could look," said Eddie. "I don't intend trying to buy or eat anything."

Len burst into a ghostly laugh.

"I'd like to see you try! If it's like everything else, your hands wouldn't be able to pick anything up. Think about it – you're a ghost! And as for trying to swallow something, well, the mind just boggles at the thought!"

"Yeah, but there are such things as poltergeists, you know. They can make things move and jump about. That would be fun to try in a big department store. We could scare people witless. I bet I could do it."

Len thought for a moment, searching the remnants of his human mind. After a brief pause, he said,

"Well, we could head north for Regent's Park where I can show you the zoo and on the way we can go down Oxford Street where you can visit Selfridge's or John Lewis for your little games."

Len's fairly accurate knowledge of London suggested to Eddie that Len had done some homework before they had met up a few minutes earlier. After all, Len had only been eight when he had left Whitechapel in the East End. What Eddie wasn't aware of at that moment was that his friend wanted to try an unusual and outrageous experiment when he got to London Zoo.

"Let's go, then," said Eddie.

"Right you are, Captain. Follow me."

The boys headed away from the midday sun and, at the north end of the square, Len took them left past the National Gallery. A poster advertising the latest exhibition confirmed to them that the year was indeed 1967 and also that the month was probably August, judging by the dates printed thereon. Up the Haymarket they glided, Eddie soon learning that, like Len, he could move more quickly and smoothly with a little practice. Within five minutes, they had reached the bustling and colourful Picadilly Circus and, continuing north, they were soon at the lower end of Regents Street where Len paused to let Eddie catch up.

"Hamley's toy shop is up ahead on the right. Want to look in there, mate?" asked Len.

"No, Len. You are forgetting that we would have both been sixteen by now, given its August 1967. We may look like fourteen-year-olds, if, indeed, anyone could see us, but I, for one, feel that my mind has aged if not my body. I'm not really interested in toys and things like train sets anymore."

"O.K., Captain. Thanks for the lecture. Straight up to Oxford Circus, then."

The two boys weaved their way through the shoppers; it was still difficult to decide whether it was a weekday or a weekend, though the likelihood of the mass protest being held mid-week seemed unlikely. On reaching Oxford Circus, Len managed to find a newspaper vendor and right under his nose he perused the day's news. He quickly found what he wanted and turned back to Eddie and announced,

"Saturday, August the 19th, 1967, mate."

"Good, it's so nice to know what day it is," said Eddie sarcastically.

Soon they were gliding down the middle of Oxford Street, heading west and letting taxis and buses run through them as they did so. Eddie was less adventurous than his friend who would try to throw his arms round any of the passengers and, in one case, round the driver himself. Eddie had still not really got used to his newly acquired freedom and steered a more modest course, even flinching if a vehicle of any shape or size came near him. He did, however, let a vicar on a bicycle ride over him; surely a man of the cloth would be the most likely person to see him if he needed to take evasive action, he thought. Suddenly, Len stopped and, pointing right, exclaimed,

"There it is – Selfridge's. One of the best shops in London and expensive, too."

"In we go, then," said Eddie.

Without fear of being seen, the two boys stayed initially on the ground floor, pretending they could smell all the sweet vapours that the perfume counters were emitting. After a few minutes of investigation, Eddie decided on his first trick. Selecting what appeared to be the most expensive display counter, he positioned himself next to a glamorous middle-aged lady who was, with her false platinum hair, clearly dressed and painted well beyond her actual class in society. In short, she looked like a barmaid trying to be a princess. She was spraying her neck and forearms liberally with *L'Amour* and as she put the perfume bottle down, Eddie made a grab for it with his invisible hands. Just as Len had said earlier, his hand closed right round and through the bottle; it didn't diverge from its path back to the counter. Len grinned and said,

"Told you so – you're not a poltergeist yet, old boy."

Eddie wasn't about to give up, though. The lady reached for another 'tester' and just before her hand closed round the bottle, Eddie screwed up his face in concentration and stared at it without a even a hint of a ghostly blink. 'Madame Pompidour' let out a faint shriek of surprise as the bottle slid about six inches away from her. Len's jaw dropped in equal surprise. The lady reached for the bottle a second time and Eddie repeated his trick as the bottle returned to its original position. When she tried to pick it up for a third time, only for it to slide towards her and onto the floor, shattering into tiny pieces, she gave up and walked quickly away from the counter with an air of: '*It wasn't me; I never touched it*'. Later that day she would drink several more gin and tonics and eventually put the whole bizarre event down to the two or three she had had before she had entered the famous department store. While an assistant cleared away the broken glass and attempted to clean the floor of expensive perfume, Eddie was gloating and already thinking of demonstrating his new found skill elsewhere.

"There you are, Len, I *can* do it. Maybe you can, too."

Len shook his head.

"I've tried it."

"When?"

"Just then, when you did your trick. I concentrated hard to see if I could stop the bottle but I couldn't. Looks like you've got the power and I haven't. What next, then?"

"The clothing floors, I think."

"Not ladies' fashions, I hope."

Len already had visions of his friend disrobing a young lady in one of the changing rooms. If he could move a perfume bottle, he could probably (re)move someone's clothes also!

"No, don't worry – I'll stick to gents' clothing. Confuse a few old men, eh?"

Len still didn't look too happy but his friend was already heading to the escalator for the third floor where said department was located.

"Wait for me," he shouted and he just managed to catch Eddie up as he put his foot on the lowest step. Len jumped in front and said,

"I'll show you a trick, Captain. Watch this!"

Without using the handrails for support, he took two giant strides, touching the moving stairs just once on his way to the top and unaided by the motion of the escalator. In so doing, he probably broke the world long jump record, and twice at that!

Despite it being the weekend, the gents' clothing department was surprisingly quiet. The hot weather had, no doubt, a lot to do with it with traditional smart clothing not being a priority except for the more mature gentleman. Indeed, there seemed to be only two customers in view and Eddie made his mind up straightaway which one he wanted to surprise. A tall, elegant and smartly dressed man of about seventy was trying on straw hats, which judging by his lack of hair, seemed to be an absolute and immediate necessity for him, given the present weather conditions. Eddie strode up to him and from less than a yard away proceeded to stare intently at his head, now covered by the latest offering from the young male sales assistant. In no time at all, the hat dislodged itself from the old man's scalp and took off into the air as if blown there by a strong wind. The old gentleman jerked his right hand upwards in a vain attempt to stop its progress and said to the assistant,

"You must have a window open, young man. Go and close it and fetch me that hat."

The young assistant retrieved the hat and said nothing in reply about a window; he knew that there wasn't one open in his section. The old man tried the hat again. Looking in the mirror held by the sales assistant, he gave a satisfied smile at its comfortable fit and stylish looks.

"Yes, I'll take this one. How much is it, young man?"

The assistant reached up to look at the tag hanging from the brim of the hat and, just as he did so, it flew off the man's head in the opposite direction to its first journey. The customer assumed that the young assistant had been the cause when looking for the price tag and said in an angry and frustrated tone,

"What are you doing, boy? Be careful, you'll ruin it."

"But, sir, I didn't touch it. You must have jerked your head suddenly."

The man had nearly had enough.

"Don't be impertinent young man. I did no such thing. Now fetch it and tell me the price."

"Yes, sir. Sorry, sir."

The hat was safely retrieved for the second time. Cash and receipt were exchanged with the old man saying,

"Thank you, young man. There's no need to wrap it – I'll wear it straightaway."

"Yes, sir," replied the bemused assistant, and the old man walked proudly away from him with his new hat firmly on his head, or so he thought. Eddie had other ideas. The man hadn't gone more than three or four paces when the hat again took off into the air but this time vertically upwards, landing neatly on an uncovered light fitting which was several feet above head height. The lightly coloured straw hat had found a new role as a makeshift light shade. Neither boy could contain himself any longer and Len croaked,

"How did you do that, mate? That was brilliant!"

"And enough fun for the time being, I think," replied Eddie. "Let's get out of here."

As the two boys turned to go they caught sight of a bewildered and extremely angry old man berating the young assistant who, with a colleague, was vainly trying to get the hat down with a long window pole, before the straw got so hot it started to smoulder.

Len still seemed to know where he was going as the two young ghosts headed out of Selfridges and back up Oxford Street, where, reaching Oxford Circus, he turned left. He was setting a furious pace as he led Eddie into Portland Place almost at a run. Crossing the Marylebone Road, he turned and said to his friend,

"That's Regent's Park ahead; I'm sure I went there with Mum and Dad when I was about six. The zoo is somewhere over to the left."

Len slowed to a normal human walking pace as they entered the Park, and Eddie could tell immediately from the high fences and other safety measures that the zoo was indeed just on their left. They made their way into the Park where Eddie began to dawdle while his eyes were taken by all the sunbathing young ladies who were sporting themselves on the grass in the sun.

"Come on, Eddie, there's no need for that," said Len. "Remember, you're only fourteen and not supposed to be interested in members of the opposite sex; you turned down Sally Barber's invitation on the day before you departed your previous life."

Eddie looked wistful, trying to hard to recall what his friend was talking about, but his memory was hazy and disjointed. Sally had been a new girl to Fenton Grammar's fourth year and had taken to supporting him in his worse subject, English, by sitting next to him in most of the lessons. He shook his ghostly body and joined Len in looking for their planned destination. Some strange and somewhat frightening animal noises could now be heard from behind the boundary fence to their left. Eddie stopped walking for a moment.

"What's that?"

"Only the lions or tigers, mate."

Eddie looked around nervously, as if said animals might actually be roaming free within Regent's Park. Len reassured him.

64

"Don't worry, Captain, they're kept securely locked in pens and cages."

Eddie relaxed a bit; animals were not among his favourite things after a nasty experience with a dog when he had been seven.

"Thank God for that," he said.

They followed the boundary fence right round to the main entrance at the north side of the zoo. Eddie gasped at the entry prices but Len remarked at once,

"What's the problem, mate? We ain't gonna pay."

Len led the way straight through one of the turnstiles and into the main concourse. The zoo was packed with tourists eager to see what strange and exotic creatures lay within her tall fences.

"Where to first, comrade?" asked Eddie.

"Lions and tigers, I think. Kill or cure your fear of animals, eh?"

Following the signs past the gorillas and the picnic areas, they came across the tigers near the southern end of the zoo. A magnificent male lay basking in the early afternoon sun; the head of his female counterpart could just be seen poking out of a wooden cage at the rear of the pen.

"Wow!" whispered Eddie. "They're huge."

"And kill you in seconds if they got out," replied his friend.

Eddie failed to see the funny side of Len's ridiculous words and backed away from the pen until Len then said,

"Oh come on, Eddie, get real – I think you're safe, aren't you? You can't die twice and, anyway, you're invisible."

Invisible they might have been but something was happening inside the tiger's pen. A small crowd had gathered as the lioness joined her mate and then both animals came over to stand inches from the boys on the other side of the metal fence. Simultaneously, they leapt at the fence, each with a tremendous roar and mouth wide open to show their massive and incredible teeth. Several people, who had been standing a good distance away, jumped in terror at the tiger's unusual behaviour and the frightening sound of the metal fence being shook with almost unearthly force. From out of the shade a keeper came running. The roar and the fence rattling were repeated. Some of the crowd gasped. The keeper seemed angry and, as he stood right between the two mesmerised ghosts, he said,

"Who did it? Who's upset Solomon and Sheba?"

No one moved or said a word. No one had been within ten yards of the pen before the animals went into their rage, only …. The keeper made strange, but obviously comforting noises, and the two lions returned quietly to their former peaceful states. Eddie and Len had backed away behind the gathering crowd and the younger ghost was first to speak.

"They sensed us, didn't they, Len?"

"I don't know, mate. I mean, how could they?"

"Because they have different senses to us – same way that some cats apparently know when their owners are about to be ill, I suppose."

Eddie paused and then said,

"Is that why you wanted to bring me here? To show me that?"

"No, I wanted to do something much more dangerous, or, at least, unusual."

"What?"

"I'll show you at a different pen."

"Where?"

"I don't know yet. Let's just have a look round at the other animals. There are loads to see."

"Something a little less scary, please," begged Eddie.

"How about the monkey house?"

"I suppose so. As long as they're small and timid."

The monkey house appeared to be only a bit further on at the very southernmost extremity of the zoo and the two boys reached it at a slow walk in a couple of minutes, with Eddie steering a course down the middle of the pathways. They approached with caution, but the several different types of apes and monkeys carried on with their normal business, seeming not to notice the two ghost's presence outside their cages.

"All seems fine," said Len. "Looks like they can't sense us."

Eddie moved closer to Len who was standing right next to the cage.

"Ugh! Look at that one's red bum," said Eddie, "and that one has got his thing out!"

While Eddie continued to stare at the monkey's strange anatomy and behaviour, Len moved a few feet away from his friend. Eddie immediately sensed that Len was going to do the 'something' he had been promising to do since they entered the zoo. It also seemed that he didn't want Eddie to try and dissuade him from so doing, though what Eddie could have done, short of remonstrating and shouting some silent and ghostly words, was a complete mystery to him. Suddenly Len moved forwards and passed right into the monkey's cage. Still the animals carried on with their 'monkey business'. To Eddie's horror, Len walked right up to a male and female orang-utan who were picking insects out of each other's coarse hair and plonked himself down in front them. Eddie tried to mouth some words but his throat had gone dry; a meaningless gasp was all he could muster. A few seconds went by and Eddie became a bit more relaxed about the situation. Len, of course, was right, what could the apes to do to them? But the sight of his best friend sitting between two sizeable orang-utans was, nevertheless, still not easy to come to terms with. Both weighed over ten stone and were prone to avoid human contact – Eddie had already read the sign fixed to their cage. Len grinned cheekily at his friend and called out,

"This is was what I was going to try with the tigers, mate!"

Eddie gave a nervous wave but did not reply. Suddenly, the male orang-utan looked fidgety, rocking from side to side on its haunches and uttering a high-pitched screeching noise. Len turned round and looked up into the ape's reddish-brown and heavily-set face. As he did so, the orang-utan *appeared* to place its right hand squarely on Len's head and began to gently stroke and lift his blond hair. A few seconds later the female did likewise with her left hand. Eddie couldn't stand it any longer.

"Please come out, Len!"

Len seemed to agree with his friend's request. He got to his feet and walked calmly through the wire cage front and back onto the pathway. He immediately called to Eddie.

"That was fun, Captain. You see, we can do things now that living people are not allowed to do."

"Or want to do," called back Eddie.

Len wandered the few yards back to stand beside his friend and immediately Eddie's face went a shade whiter than his normal ghostly colour.

"Len! Your hair! Look at your hair!"

Len moved to a glass-fronted cage a short distance away and looked at his reflection. He could hardly believe his eyes when he discovered his hair had taken on a 'Ken Dodd' appearance, and after an electric shock at that. Though no one could see him, his ghostly mind still possessed some vanity and he hurriedly tried to hand brush it back into something resembling his usual appearance. He returned to Eddie with a quizzical look upon his face.

"Well, explain that, will you?"

Eddie shook his head in disbelief.

"Impossible, Len – just impossible. How could a living, breathing animal ruffle your hair like that when you're a ghost? It's just not possible, mate."

For the first time for a while that Eddie could remember, his friend seemed at a loss for words; he was genuinely puzzled and disconcerted.

After a short walk back to a picnic area situated roughly in the middle of the zoo complex, the two boys sat down on the grass next to a family with two young children. Even Len now seemed to prefer the predictability of humans. They hadn't spoken much on the way there.

"They must have touched you," said Eddie at last. "Didn't you feel anything? Your hair couldn't have got into that state without you feeling something, surely."

Len shook his head.

"No, not as much as to make it such a mess. I did think there was a light breeze, but that's all."

Eddie had obviously been thinking deeply about the significance of the event when he then said,

"I wonder if it means that we can do the same to people or animals."

"We haven't tried anything yet, have we?" replied Len. "The trick in Selfridge's was done without contact."

"Yeah but that was an inanimate object."

Len shook his head again.

"But we've walked straight through living people and them through us and neither of us felt anything or disturbed anyone."

"Maybe we have to concentrate, like when I concentrated on the perfume bottle."

Len moved himself a few feet away from Eddie as the two young children began to pick daisies right next to him. Eddie followed, and they spent some time in silence just watching the two little girls, one blond and aged about seven and one aged a year or two younger with curly ginger hair that matched his own. Eddie recalled the times when he had been about the younger girl's age, and all the teasing or even name-calling he used to suffer because his hair colour stood him out from the crowd – he had been the only one in his class of thirty at Fenton Central Junior School. He wondered if the little girl had already faced similar teasing and how she would cope with it. While Eddie was thinking wistfully about his own childhood, the children's parents began to pack their picnic away, the mother calling to her offspring,

"Maggie, Hilary, time to go. Come and help tidy up, please."

The older girl was quick to her feet and went over to her mother and proudly presented her with the daisy chain she had just made. The younger one seemed content to lie on the grass in the sunshine. Eddie smiled as he could see how she was trying to avoid having to help her big sister. Eddie's sister had often got out of the washing up after a Sunday lunch with a similar tactic – retiring to her bedroom and pretending to be asleep with a headache had worked on several occasions in the Compton household. Mother called again,

"Maggie, will you please come and help otherwise there will be no ice-cream for you, my girl!"

Maggie got slowly and reluctantly to her feet and sulked her way over to her sister where she then made minimal effort to assist. Her dad patted her on her head and she clung to him for protection as her big sister began shouting at her.

"She always gets away with it, Mum and I …."

Eddie didn't really concentrate on the rest of the argument that was starting as he had glanced at his friend who seemed to be drifting off to sleep. Len looked tired after his 'brush' with the orang-utans. In no time at all, his image started to fade and then he was suddenly gone. Eddie's friend had gone back to 'sleep' and he was alone again.

That day had provided a quick learning experience for Eddie and Len as trainee ghosts and, as he made his way back out of the zoo with no particular purpose in mind, Eddie pondered his progress. Several questions came to him in the afternoon sunshine. Did everyone end up as a ghost or was the experience only given to a chosen few? If everyone who died did become a ghost, why hadn't he and Len seen any others yet, apart, that was, from a few familiar faces? There would have to be billions, if not trillions, of ghosts wandering the earth from the beginning of time, if everybody became one. His poltergeist trick hadn't been that difficult to perform, he thought and yet it had always seemed to him that it would have been an extremely rare 'event' in real life, if such things ever happened at all. That, on the other hand, meant that ghosts like him and his friend might be extremely rare. However, as he left London Zoo that afternoon, he didn't reach a satisfactory conclusion, torn as he was between thinking that he was in elite company, or that he was merely one of an unimaginable host who remained unaware of one another, until something or someone forced their paths to cross.

Although Eddie made it safely out of the zoo and some way back towards the city's West End shopping area, he, like his friend, soon became tired and this time his visit to the real world finished abruptly while he was still walking. He felt warm inside (?) as he disappeared back into oblivion.

6

Wedding Day

Plans for Jenny's and Gary's wedding had gone well so far during the first half of 1968 and the all-important day was fast approaching as the final pieces of the jigsaw were being put in place. The stag and hen nights had been arranged for Thursday, September the 12th, with the big day arranged for the Saturday that week. Both young people had the following week off; Jenny from her job at 'Curls and Twirls', the hairdressing salon in Hamsden and Gary from the local fire service. In her year at the salon since leaving college, Jenny had worked hard and had already risen to the manager's number two. The honeymoon was to be taken in London. Gary, courtesy of his parent's generosity, had booked a reasonably expensive hotel in the West End for four nights, while the remainder of the week was scheduled for more cleaning and decorating at their newly acquired flat in Hamsden. It overlooked one of the main squares in the centre of town and was perfect, Gary had decided, for going on nights out, with cinemas, restaurants and pubs within a stone's throw of the front door of their ground floor apartment.

In the intervening months since the ghostly encounter with her brother, Jenny had not experienced any further such events. Yes, she had had strange dreams, but nothing remotely similar to something where she had actually been awake and talking to him. Indeed, even memories of that single event had begun to recede and, at times, she had come to question what had really taken place. Her father, too, had not had any other visions since the one at Wembley Stadium over two years previously. He and his daughter had had the occasional conversation about Eddie and, though nothing has ever been said between them, there did seem to be a tacit understanding that they each knew more than they

72

were prepared to let on. Father's knew their daughters and daughters their fathers more deeply than most people might imagine. One such conversation actually occurred on the very morning of September the 14th, just as Jenny and her mother were going to start the preparations for the day. The two of them were alone in the lounge with Fred Compton going through the arrangements for the day with his daughter. His fastidious approach with timings and events often spilled over into his private life, too.

"What time is the car coming?"

Jenny sighed. She knew her dad of old.

"You know what time, Dad – quarter to eleven."

"Are you sure that gives us enough time, Jenny?"

"The driver says so and he should know; I mean he must have done hundreds of weddings at St Andrew's and it's only a five or ten minute drive from here – you should know that. You and Mum have done it enough times."

"But the wedding is at eleven – we may have less than five minutes when we get there; the bridesmaids have got to be organised and your dress straightened for the procession into the church and down the aisle."

"Oh, for goodness sake, stop fussing! What does it matter if I'm late? It's the bride's prerogative."

But Fred Compton wouldn't let up – he had to let his nervousness out somehow, and his daughter was bearing the brunt of his anxiousness.

"The Reverend Weaver said that there's another wedding scheduled for twelve."

Jenny had had enough.

"Dad! Shut up!"

She got up from her chair and went over to her father and kissed him lightly on his forehead and said,

"Just calm down, Dad. Everything will be fine. I want you and Mum to relax and just enjoy the day – you deserve it after all the help you've given me and Gary, especially with the deposit on the flat. It's going to be a perfect day; perfect in every way except for …."

Jenny paused and looked wistfully out of the window. Her dad seemed to understand.

"I know, love, but Eddie will be looking down on you in spirit. Maybe he'll be there."

Jenny was about to burst into tears but her father's words had struck a different chord at that moment of charged emotions.

"What do you mean, Dad?"

Fred Compton realised he had chosen the wrong time to discuss his deeper thoughts and said hurriedly,

"I didn't mean literally, love – just in our hearts and minds."

Jenny then let her emotions go and, hugging her dad, the tears rolled down her cheeks. Fred Compton, too, had wet eyes when his daughter eventually stood up.

"Now go and get ready and make me the proudest father alive," he said, gently patting her hand.

"Thanks, Dad. I will try."

As she joined her mum for all her necessary facial preparations, Jenny was left thinking that the tacit understanding had started to become a little more concrete between father and daughter.

St Andrew's was pretty full for the wedding of Jennifer Olivia Compton and Gary Steven Jones; Mr Richard Jones was well-known in the area, despite his dubious occupation as a second-hand car dealer. It was mostly unwarranted – Fred Compton had himself bought his latest car from Gary's father and had had absolutely no problems with it over the three years he had owned it. Fred Compton, too, was well-liked in Fenton-on-Sea and the Comptons as a family had often been in people's thoughts since their son had gone missing over two and half years ago. Many people had thought that the Compton's fate had been worse than if their son had been confirmed dead and they had buried his body. They were still in limbo and his disappearance was still listed as: '*Missing, presumed dead*'.

Jenny looked absolutely stunning as she walked up the aisle with her father. Her long white flowing dress had been selected from the best bridal shop in the area and it fitted and suited her to a tee. She had allowed her blond hair to grow to a length that required careful pinning to get her headdress to fit properly and securely. Even unromantic Gary gave an inward gasp when he glanced over his shoulder and saw her for the first time in all her wedding-day beauty. Halfway down the aisle, her father whispered,

"You look absolutely beautiful, Jenny. I'm so proud of you, love."

"*So am I, big sister.*"

"Thanks, Dad."

"*Yeah, well done, Dad.*"

Fred Compton felt his daughter stiffen, but he immediately put it down to Jenny's nervousness as she approached the altar and the love of her life. That wasn't the reason, however, as Jenny had glimpsed something out of her right eye – someone else was walking beside her up the aisle! Unnoticed to begin with, Eddie, dressed in his Sunday best, had accompanied his sister on her right side all the way from the time she and her father had entered the church. Jenny's body and dress had hid him from her father's view, if, indeed, he had been given the privilege to see or hear his son. He hadn't.

Understandably, Jenny was considerably apprehensive when she eventually stood side by side with Gary and the age-old ceremony began. When it came to her turn to express her vows, she had to concentrate doubly hard on her carefully rehearsed words.

"I, Jennifer Olivia Compton …."

"*I Jennifer Olivia Compton*," mimicked Eddie from his position still at her side, his interruption sounding like an echo in his sister's head.

"…. take you, Gary Steven Jones, to be my lawful wedded husband, to have and to hold from this day forward …."

"*Are you really sure, Jen. You can still change your mind.*"

"…. for better or for worse, for richer, for poorer …."

"*Take his money, sis.*"

"…. in sickness and in health, to love and to cherish …."

"*Well, O.K., if you're really sure.*"

"…. from this day forward until death do us part."

"*Well I guess that's that, then.*"

Then the young couple's day took a real turn for the worse. For her part, Jenny had managed her vows superbly, notwithstanding the ghostly comments from her dear departed brother. However, when it came for the best man to provide the ring, Eddie exercised his role as a poltergeist by projecting it from his open palm straight into a vase full of water and assorted flowers. Gary murmured something to his best school friend about trying not to be so nervous, having naturally assumed that the ring's flight had been due to sweaty and trembling hands, or even the three stiff whiskies earlier. It then took a few minutes for the ring to be retrieved; the vase had to be emptied into another and the flowers similarly redistributed. Eddie made himself scarce among the congregation, in case his sister should have put two and two together. His next trick could take place from a distance, he thought.

All was well until the couple came to make their walk back down the aisle. With all eyes now fixed firmly on the happy pair, Eddie performed his caper. He had noticed one of his little cousins standing right at the end of a row of pews next to the side of the aisle down which Gary was about to walk. Just as the proud new husband passed the smiling blond-haired boy, Eddie 'persuaded' him to stick out a leg and trip him up. Gary catapulted forward, catching his foot in Jenny's dress which ripped with a loud noise. He ended up in an undignified prostrate position on the floor. He got to his feet as quickly and in as dignified way as possible and, fortunately, found himself to be unscathed. The only real damage was to his pride and his wife's dress. Fortunately, the ripped garment had seemed to be the least of Jenny's worries when she helped him to his feet. There was, of course, some inevitable laughter and comment, particularly from some of Gary's fire service colleagues.

"*Call yourself a fireman!*"

"*How many have you had, Jonesey?*"

"*Under the wife's thumb already, mate?*"

Eddie was also laughing, in his ghostly way and, unnoticed by anyone, he was already climbing into the back seat of his dad's Hillman Minx. He wasn't going to miss the reception at the Marine Hotel set in the beautiful cliff gardens at the top of East Hill.

The Marine Hotel was the plushest such establishment in Fenton-on-Sea, and its booking had only been enabled with a substantial contribution from Gary's parents. Richard Jones had also provided the bride's car without charge, a vintage white Rolls Royce which was part of his normal hire fleet. It was a modest gathering – about sixty guests had been invited, and the reception lunch was to be held in the East Room, a superb open-plan area decorated and furnished in the art deco style of the twenties.

The addition of large potted palms gave the room a definite continental feel. By the time all the introductions and handshaking had taken place, Eddie was already in his place behind one such palm. He still possessed doubts at times that he would remain invisible, particularly as his sister had been able to see him, but he had no immediate plans to disturb the gathering that afternoon. He just wanted to watch the proceedings out of general interest and to be able to discuss them with his sister should he want to at some time in the future. Len would have called it a 'watching brief'.

The meal was quite an opulent affair with five courses, smoked salmon, prime rib of beef and Black Forest gateau being three of the most popular choices. Jenny had begun to relax as soon as she and Gary had climbed into their white Rolls outside the church; memories of the mishaps there seemed to have been forgotten. Though she knew that her brother had been with her up to and including the time when she had said her vows, she was still totally unaware of his involvement in the two 'pranks' afterwards. She had put the accidents down to nervousness on both the best man's and her new husband's part. She was strangely both relieved and disappointed that Eddie hadn't seemed to have followed her to the hotel, and she heard no phantom interruptions to any of the speeches that followed the meal. She knew that both her dad and Gary had been very nervous about delivering their contributions in front of an audience that contained many strangers to each of them. In her mind and known only to her, Jenny's day had been made all the more perfect by her brother's ghostly visit, albeit in somewhat awkward circumstances. Despite his continual and comical interruptions, she had felt a warmness and contentment that he had given his blessing to their union. Gary Jones hadn't always been accepted by her brother as she still remembered quite well.

By three-thirty, the photographer had begun to take some rather more informal shots than those of the wedding party and guests that he'd taken earlier outside the church. The warm late summer sunshine showed the cliff top gardens off to perfection, with the deep blue sea in the background. Mr Ralph Hollister was at liberty to show off his artistic skills. He started with the newly-wed couple, before they went off to change into something less formal for the evening disco and party, scheduled to start at seven. A taxi had been booked to take them to their London hotel at eight-thirty. He appeared satisfied with the first three shots he took with the North Sea in the background, but suddenly became annoyed when he asked the couple to face out to sea. The art deco architecture of the Marine Hotel, lit by the brilliant afternoon sun, provided a romantic background which he didn't want to miss.

"Please get out of the shot, young man," shouted Ralph Hollister with some irritation. A look of confusion spread across Gary's face when he looked about and saw no one fitting the photographer's description within twenty yards of the scene. Jenny looked more apprehensive than confused as she, too, glanced round. No, Eddie didn't seem to be there, she thought. Mr Hollister refocused his camera and took two quick shots of the happy couple. After a few minutes, the photographer left Gary and Jenny to themselves and she pre-empted Gary's inevitable question by saying,

"It must have been one of my young cousins messing about. He probably ran behind us just as Mr Hollister was going to take the picture."

The incident clearly hadn't concerned Gary as much as Jenny thought it might have done when he replied,

"What, love? Yes, you're probably right – these budding David Baileys can be very sensitive."

Jenny suspected that there *had* been a young man attempting to join in their photo session and, of course, she knew it hadn't been one of her cousins.

A few days later, when Mr Hollister developed his photographs from the Compton-Jones wedding, he would discover to his annoyance that three of his shots had been ruined by the addition of a grinning teenage boy dressed in a smart suit. In one – taken with the hotel in the background – he was standing right between the happy couple, with arms folded over his chest which was stuck out like a soldier on parade. Needless to say, Mr Hollister destroyed the offending photographs and accompanying negatives, so that Eddie's final little trick was thwarted at the last moment. It would have to remain an unanswered question as to what Jenny or Gary or the rest of their families would have done if the photographs had reached public circulation. If Mr Ralph Hollister had possessed an inquiring mind, bordering on the scientific or detective, he might have searched through the other hundred or so photographs to see if he could identify the object of his annoyance, but, being of the more artistic temperament, Eddie's concrete images were lost forever.

7

Moon Dance

Eddie had thoroughly enjoyed the day at his sister's wedding. Whoever or whatever was now in charge of his 'life' – whether the God he had begun to trust, or some other natural phenomenon – his silent prayers had been answered. He had seen Jenny get married and had had some fun at her and Gary's expense, too. Annoying the photographer had suggested, however, that it was not only friends and family that might be allowed to see him; he had sensed that neither Jenny nor Gary had been aware of his presence at that time. As he wandered alone, and once more invisible in the cliff top gardens, he amused himself thinking about the prospect of his family getting the photographs back with his cheeky face staring at them from some of them. He knew it shouldn't be possible, but, given everything else that had happened, you just never knew ….

It was getting quite late when Eddie began to feel the inevitable tiredness creep up on him. The last thing he would see that day would be a beautiful harvest moon rising over the sea and his last thought would be about how huge and close it seemed to be.

The new Mr and Mrs Jones made their taxi to London and spent a gloriously happy honeymoon there. It would not be long before the seeds of the next generation would be sown and by the following July, Jenny announced to Gary that she was pregnant. Fortunately, number 4A Beaumont Square, Hamsden was a two-bedroom flat and they would spend the next few months getting it ready for the new arrival(s) due at the end of the year, 1969.

It was to be after his sister's news had been made public that Eddie would be awakened again; this time, also, he would soon be joined by his best friend. Loud and raucous noises greeted him before he was allowed the power of sight. Unfamiliar noises – car horns, people shouting in English but with a strange twang – greeted his ears.

"Watch it, bud!"

"Can't you learn to drive, lady?"

"The sidewalks are for walking on, fella!"

Eddie's eyes opened slowly. It appeared to be fairly early in the morning, judging by the long shadows being cast by the sun. He found himself in a wide thoroughfare, lined on each side with expensive looking shops. Strange cars were rushing by him, big and futuristic looking, many being coloured a bright and garish shade of yellow with black letters printed on their sides. He was in the middle of the road and he began to panic momentarily until he remembered what powers he possessed. At first he thought he was viewing the scene in a mirror as things seemed to be the wrong way round. Then he realised that it was the cars that were causing the illusion – each line of traffic was being driven on the wrong side of the road! He moved carefully to the pavement and from his position further back from the cars, he was able to read the lettering on one of the yellow cars:

'New York Cab Co.'

So that was it, he thought – the good ol' U S of A and the capital at that, the Big Apple. This was exciting. As a ghost it seemed he could cross boundaries, oceans and time zones. The question was: Why? Why New York? As he dawdled along the pavement (sidewalk), he also wondered if Len was going to join him on what was clearly a new and different adventure. That it was morning was quickly confirmed by looking at the faces of the businessmen hurrying to their offices. They did not have the relaxed looks of men who had just completed a good and tiring days' work. Neon signs off all colours flashed all around him and looking up, he realised the main reason for the long shadows, which, in some cases darkened the entire road. Skyscrapers reached into the sky, blocking the sun from casting its warming rays on the scene below. One of the neon signs confirmed the exact date and time to Eddie: July 16th, 08:52. The year was a little bit more difficult to ascertain. Eddie's ghostly mind, though not as good as a human one at remembering things, did allow him, in this case, to recall that it had been September 1968 the last time he had been awake. A newspaper stand quickly provided the answer: 1969 and, apart from gleaning the date, Eddie was astonished to read the headline of one of the papers.

'MAN TAKES OFF FOR THE MOON TODAY
Apollo 11 all set for launch this morning'

Eddie took a ghostly step backwards – surely it couldn't be possible? He did remember back when he'd been alive that there had been talk of putting a man on the moon by the end of the decade, but he had hardly believed it – something to do with a speech by the late President John Kennedy. And here he was in the very country that was going to attempt such an incredible feat. Eddie was excited. His visit surely had to have something to do with it. Where was the launch to take place? New York? No, that couldn't be right – it was Cape Canaveral in Florida where all the other space rockets had lifted off. His immediate thoughts, however, were disturbed by a familiar voice which spoke in a fake American accent.

"*Hi there, buddy! Welcome to the land of the free.*"

Unlike the previous time in Fenton-on-Sea, Eddie was caught off guard and forgot to check the identity of the person to whom the voice belonged. His excitement at waking up in New York on such a momentous day had led his mind elsewhere. When he turned round to see his possible friend, he even failed to notice that 'Len' did not ask the relevant question either.

"Hi ya, Len. What's up?"

"Not much, Compo, just doing some jaywalking. It's good fun to do it here because it's actually an offence, you know. I've been having quite a blithe time."

And then it hit Eddie like an arrow right between the eyes which pierced his head with the cold, hard realisation of his mistake. This 'Len' had used the old code which he must have picked up on a previous occasion. Eddie said nothing and carried on walking for a few moments in order to see what the ghost would do. Predictably, he repeated the question.

"I said: I've had a *blithe* time."

"Have you really? So what?"

"So, aren't you going to check something out with me, Ed?"

"Don't call me Ed, please."

"Don't call me Ed, please," mimicked the evil ghost. "Ooh, aren't we the touchy one?"

Eddie got more confident.

"Go away! Just, go away and leave me alone."

"Go away? I'm not going anywhere, sunshine. I'm going to be bad, oh, so bad."

Another familiar voice entered the conversation from somewhere to Eddie's left.

"Run, Eddie! Run!"

Without stopping to check where the new voice had come from, Eddie propelled himself forward in a straight line and ran as fast as he could, straight through several pedestrians until he reached a wider stretch of sidewalk where there were fewer people about. He looked nervously behind him and was partially relieved to see only one familiar person who was strolling nonchalantly in his direction. Coming up close, 'Len' said,

"He nearly got you, mate."

Eddie folded his arms and stared back at the ghost.

"Ask me the question, Len, please?"

"What question?"

"You tell me, comrade."

The ghost looked thoughtful.

"Well, let me see. How about, what's the capital of France? No – not that one? Well, what about, the capital of England? No, that's wrong, too. Oh, I don't know. What do you want me to ask you?"

Eddie turned to run again but then the ghost said,

"Only kidding, Captain. What *is* the twentieth prime number?

Eddie was still not sure and said,

"Well, that would be seventy-three, I do believe."

"Oh, very clever, Eddie. Now give me the correct answer."

Eddie smiled.

"No, *you* give the real answer."

"O.K., if you wish, but I have to say that you're being just a teeny bit pedantic, mate. The correct answer, as you well know, is seventy-one."

"Thank God; it is you, Len."

"Indeed, my friend. I'd have thought you would have realised that when I knew the right question to ask, but you can't be ...."

Eddie finished Len's sentence.

"Too careful? You're damn right I am, comrade Len."

By now the two boys had reached what seemed to be a major intersection of roads and Len pointed to a sign high up on an adjacent building.

"Look, we're at Fifth Avenue and Times Square."

Eddie didn't seem to be that interested in their location and replied, "You know what's happening today, don't you."

Len expressed his ignorance of the moon shot.

"No – should I?"

Then Eddie told him, in as calm a manner as possible, about the headline he had read earlier and his passive excitement suddenly became much more animated when passed to his friend, who said,

"Wow! Where? We've got to go and see it."

Even when his friend informed him that the launch was scheduled to be at least a thousand miles further south in Florida, Len's excitement did not abate.

"So? We can get there – hopping on trains and planes is not a problem for us. Won't cost us anything and when we get close we'll just follow the crowds. There must be thousands going."

Len's normal down-to-earth approach had made the problem seem so easy until Eddie really brought him *down to earth*.

"Yeah, but the paper said that the Saturn Five rocket is due to take off at about nine-thirty this morning and the time has already got to be past nine o'clock."

"Ten past, to be precise, Captain," replied Len, looking at a huge clock hanging above Times Square. He was not to be beaten as he then said,

"Still no problem – we'll just think our way there. After all, someone must have landed us here on today of all days for a reason, don't you think?"

Eddie had been thinking more or less the same thing just before he met his friend and replied,

"I'm game if you are. Who's going to do the thinking?"

"We both will. On the count of three we both start concentrating on …."

Len paused and said,

"Where is it?"

"Kennedy Space Centre at Cape Canaveral in Florida," said Eddie.

"On three, then. Ready? One – two – three – go!"

Eddie didn't have time to do anything but blindly follow Len's command and as soon as he said 'three', he screwed up his face and concentrated on their proposed destination, hoping that God would take control of their improbable mission.

"This is Apollo Saturn launch control. We've passed the six-minute mark in our countdown for Apollo 11, now five minutes, 52 seconds and counting. We're on time at the present time for our planned lift-off at 32 minutes past the hour. Spacecraft test conductor Skip Chauvin now has completed the status check of his personnel in the control room ….'

The monotone voice of the Launch Control Announcer droned on to the world-wide television audience as the two boy-ghosts found themselves in a location where no one on earth could ever have imagined another normal human could be at that particular time. There were already, of course, three people in the location where Eddie's and Len's ghosts found themselves – Neil Armstrong, Michael Collins and Edwin 'Buzz' Aldrin.

"T minus five minutes and counting …."

The two ghosts had no trouble fitting into the space capsule as their invisibility allowed them to roam free and, though they could see and hear each other, none of the three astronauts had the same privilege.

"*T minus four minutes and counting ….*"

"Can you believe this, Eddie?" asked Len, after both boys had regained some sort of ghostly composure.

"Yep, we're going to the moon, mate," replied Eddie grinning from ear to ear. "We can float where we want."

Eddie and Len had taken up positions with their backs to the instrument panels and seemed to be able to hover there unaided. The astronaut's view would not be blocked – ghosts didn't need space to occupy!

"I may try going outside later on," said Len, boldly.

Eddie pulled a face. His friend could not be serious, surely!

"*T minus one minute 54 seconds and counting …. Our status board indicates that the oxidiser tanks of the second and third stages have pressurised ….*"

"Well, what could go wrong, Eddie?" queried Len.

"Not much, I suppose. You might just float away into space and have to wander the infinite universe forever. Apart from that it should be plain sailing!"

"I'll just keep in contact with the capsule."

Eddie burst out laughing.

"How, sunshine? What will you use to cling on with? Your hands won't work, you idiot."

"Well, whatever or whoever has got us here and keeps us in the capsule will keep me fixed to it if I'm outside. I mean, I won't need oxygen, will I?"

"Who's to say that God will allow you to stay in contact if you try something daft like that?"

"So he's in charge, then, is he?" asked Len.

"Someone is."

"*T minus 50 seconds and counting …. Neil Armstrong just reported back it's been a real smooth countdown ….*"

"Yeah, I suppose you're right," said Len reluctantly. "Don't worry, I'll behave, mate."

"Good, now get ready," replied Eddie.

"*T minus 15 seconds …. Guidance is internal, twelve … eleven … ten ….*"

"See you in space," said Len.

"*… nine … eight … seven … ignition sequence starts, six … five … four … three … two … one … zero, all engines running. Lift-off, we have a lift-off, thirty-two minutes past the hour, lift-off on Apollo eleven.*"

Though Eddie and Len might have been subjected to some incredible noises and vibrations in the next few minutes, their ghostly ears and bodies were able to withstand them in comfort. Of course, no oxygen or similar protections were necessary as they floated around the cabin, watching in awe at the culmination of man's ingenuity and technological progress.

One minute into take-off, the three crew members were experiencing forces in excess of 3g and the Saturn Five rocket began to disappear from view beyond any cloud cover, leaving a trail of exhaust gases and a sound like rolling thunder. In less than four minutes, the Command and Service Module completed its final separation from the top of the massive Saturn rocket and the three-plus-two astronauts were left isolated in the CSM, on course for the moon. By the time the CSM had stabilised and the three genuine astronauts had started to carry out all the necessary checks and monitoring tasks, the two ghosts had both become drowsy. Eddie was the first to return to ghostly oblivion, followed within a few seconds by his friend. If either of them had known that they would lose 'consciousness', they would have panicked beyond belief in the realisation that they were leaving earth, maybe forever.

When they next 'awoke', Eddie and Len found themselves in a much smaller environment and accompanied by one less astronaut. Neither of them questioned how they had got to their new position, presumably unaided by human intervention – it was another reminder of their over-arching and divine guide. Unbeknown to the boys, 'Buzz' Aldrin and Neil Armstrong were already focusing on the necessary tasks to land the Lunar Module on the moon's surface. The LM, *Eagle*, was small and compact inside and the two ghosts were forced to merge into one entity, even though it was probably unnecessary given their ethereal nature. Like Siamese twins, they could not see each other and, in addition, talking gave them each the impression that the other's voice was coming from inside their own head.

"What's happening, Eddie?" asked Len, assuming his friend's superior scientific knowledge would provide an immediate answer.

"Not sure, mate – we're probably in the capsule that's going to do the landing on the moon."

"Oh, wow!" was all Len could think of to reply.

Somewhere 240,000 miles away, Mission Control was issuing continual updates to about one third of the world's population.

"This is Apollo control at 100 hours and 14 minutes. We are now less than two minutes from re-acquiring the spacecraft on the 13th

revolution …. We're presently 25 minutes from the separation burn that will be preformed by Mike Collins in the command module to give the lem and the CSM a separation of about two miles …."

"We're going down," said Eddie.

"Wow!" repeated his dumbstruck friend.

After a couple of real-time minutes, the boys sensed that *Eagle* had separated from the CSM. The announcer was trying to maintain his dignified monotone. More seconds passed.

"We are now in the approach phase … everything looking good. Altitude 5,200 feet …. Altitude forty-two hundred feet …."

Then one of the astronauts spoke.

"… 400 feet, down at 9 … 8 forward … You're pegged on horizontal velocity …."

Seconds later, 'Buzz' Aldrin continued,

"Altitude velocity light, three and a half down, 220 feet … 100 feet three and a half down, nine forward … 5 per cent fuel remaining … things looking good … forty feet, down … picking up some dust …."

Then Neil Armstrong called out the words that would become some of the most quoted ever with regard to space travel.

"Houston, Tranquillity base here. The Eagle had landed."

Eruptions of spontaneous applause and cheering from Mission Control could be heard all around the world as Armstrong's words were received.

"Roger Tranquillity, we copy you on the ground. You've got a bunch of guys about to turn blue; we're breathing again, thanks a lot."

Though neither ghost could see the other, each of their faces was rigid with excitement and anticipation and Eddie managed at last to speak with a note of caution in case his friend started to take things into his own hands.

"Wait, Len. Please don't try and walk through the sides of the module. Just follow the astronauts out when they are ready."

It appeared, from the movement within the module, that Armstrong and Aldrin had been on the moon for some time. The boys noticed that both men had donned extra equipment, including what appeared to be tightly fitting suits that consisted of several layers of an aluminium coloured reflective material.

"They won't get far in those," remarked Len.

"You're forgetting that there's very little gravity on the moon, mate. They'll be almost weightless like they were earlier," said Eddie.

"Will we be, too?" asked Len.

"That remains to be seen, but I think that would be possible, don't you?" laughed Eddie. "We're weightless already!"

"Hm, could be interesting," said Len.

Just then, the two men moved towards the hatch door and, after decompressing the LM, they pried the hatch open. Neil Armstrong was the first to back out of the module and onto the top of the lander's ladder. He quickly deployed a TV camera which was focused on the ladder and the first black and white pictures of the moon were transmitted back to earth. Armstrong started a running commentary as he descended the ladder.

"I'm at the foot of the ladder … the surface appears to be very, very fine grained … it's almost like powder. I'm going to step off the lem now …."

Although Mission Commander Neil A Armstrong would be the first human being to set foot on the moon, he wasn't the second 'being' to follow him. One Leonard Wilby preceded the Lunar Module Pilot, Edwin 'Buzz' Eugene Aldrin Jr., by a couple of seconds as, ignoring Eddie's earlier request, he leapt/floated down to the moon's surface to stand proudly by Commander Armstrong as he uttered the historic words:

"That's one small step for man … one giant leap for mankind."

"That was one very easy step for us ghosts … one tiny jump for ghostkind," mimicked Len. In Fenton-on-Sea, England, it was 2.56 in the early hours of the morning of Monday the 21st of July, 1969.

After a few minutes of solitary exploration by Neil Armstrong, 'Buzz' Aldrin was guided out of the module by his co-astronaut. Eddie had not appeared, much to Len's impatience, while he had stalked Neil Armstrong around the moon's surface on the first few tasks of the mission. As soon as the second astronaut reached the foot of the ladder, however, Eddie came out of the module and, like his friend almost twenty minutes earlier, he jumped and floated to the dusty surface. The dust was not disturbed in the process. Len was quick to point out how different it was for the ghosts to move around.

"Just like being on earth, Captain. We can just walk and run normally."

It was true; Eddie found that they didn't bounce over the moon's surface like the astronauts, and their movement was unencumbered by heavy moon suits and oxygen tanks. Despite his misgivings, everything seemed to be fine to Eddie and he did a little jig, causing Len to observe,

"That's quite a moon dance for you, mate."

Eddie barely heard his friend's comment as he had quickly stopped dancing to go over and read the plaque that the astronauts had just uncovered. Len joined him with two giant strides. They stood and read,

'Here Men from the Planet Earth First set Foot Upon the Moon

July 1969, AD

We Came in Peace for All Mankind'

"We came, too," said Len after a few moments.

"Yeah, along with thousands or even millions of others of our kind, eh?" remarked Eddie.

"Don't be daft," said Len. "You couldn't have got anyone else in the lunar module."

Eddie looked deprecatingly at his friend.

"I thought you were supposed to be the experienced ghost, comrade. We ghosts have other ways of moving around – we didn't have to come by rocket."

"Mm, I suppose so. Haven't seen anyone or thing that shouldn't be here, though."

Eddie's face contorted in fear.

"Well, what's that over there, then?"

Len spun round with terror etched on his face, too.

"What? Where? I don't see anything."

"Got you!" shouted Eddie, triumphantly and his friend then made a mock attempt to push him to the ground. Eddie, needlessly, backed away to avoid Len's outstretched hands. After recovering themselves, Len said,

"We could go and do some exploring – the astronauts are presumably not going back yet. They don't seem to have been here long."

Eddie glanced at the two men who were busy trying to unfurl the Stars and Stripes to leave as a permanent fixture to commemorate their visit to the moon.

"I'm not sure, Len. We should only do it if we can keep the lunar module in sight."

"O.K., but like you said, there must be other ways of getting back to earth, if, indeed, we have to go back."

"What do you mean?"

"I mean that we could stay here."

Eddie looked strangely at his friend.

"And just what would be the point of that, pray tell? There's nothing much to do up here."

Len had to agree that the lunar landscape was pretty flat and barren with few, if any, points of interest. With an unspoken agreement that they would not go out of sight of their transport, the two boys set off to explore. The light seemed to be good and they glided their way in what they thought to be the most interesting direction, dotted with small hills as it was. Not having any landmarks to judge their speed by, they covered a good distance in no time at all and without really knowing it. Eddie kept glancing over his shoulder at the lunar module, but being distracted by an interesting rock formation, he neglected to continue to do so for a couple of minutes. Eventually, Len turned round to check on their relative position and instantly exclaimed,

"It's gone – the lunar module's gone!"

Eddie turned round and gave a gasp, but then he guessed the reason.

"I forgot that the horizon is much nearer on the moon, because its diameter is only about a fifth of that of the earth, so it can be reached more quickly."

"Now you tell me!" yelled Len.

"No problem," said Eddie, reassuringly. "We'll go back now by just retracing our steps. There's obviously not much to see – it's deader than Fenton beach in winter!"

The two ghosts turned back and set off in the direction they thought the lunar module lay. Within a few hundred yards, however, it was clear to them both that they must have missed it. The 'moonlight' was fading fast, much faster than sunlight on earth and they began to panic.

This time Len seemed less concerned than his friend.

"We need some ghost tactics," he said. "We'll have to think our way there."

While Len screwed up his face in a mask of concentration, Eddie scoured the horizon for any familiar landmarks that they'd passed on their outward journey. He couldn't recognise anything and, after about five seconds, turned back to see how Len was getting on. When he did, he discovered to his horror that Len had vanished completely from off the 'face of the moon'.

"Len! Len!" he shouted.

It was getting quite dark and Eddie began to experience real panic, even though the cognitive part of his ghostly mind was telling him not to be so stupid. He began to wander blindly around, calling Len's name. Minutes passed and he was just about to give up and try to think of his next move when he thought he could just make out an object on the horizon. Running and gliding over the moon's rough surface, he reached the lunar module in less than a minute. His excitement at being back at the spacecraft was short-lived however, as the astronauts appeared to be safely locked away in their module and Len was nowhere to be seen. He felt tired and his mind didn't seem to be able process his thoughts. He called out as loudly as he could, but knew that no one could possibly hear him. He fell to his knees and prayed. He blacked out and passed once more into the safety of oblivion with his mind in turmoil as to what was going to happen to him. He hadn't thought for one moment that his friend had already preceded him by several minutes.

8

What Might Have Been

If Eddie could have felt extremes of temperature he would have been extremely hot and uncomfortable the next time he woke. Again, unusual sounds were the first signs that he had exited his slumber. Waves lapping on a beach, the rustle of trees in a gentle breeze and unfamiliar music playing from a radio in the background, formed a pleasant image in his mind's eye before his real ones opened. When they did and focused in the bright sunshine, he found himself prostrate on a sloping sandy beach of pure white and very fine sand. Shadows flicked across his eyes as he looked skywards to see the fronds of overhanging palm trees. He was somewhere exotic. He rolled over onto his side and took in the scenery. He was not quite alone, as to his right he glimpsed a heavily oiled young white-skinned couple who were sunbathing about fifty yards away. To his left, and within twenty yards, lay a single black man whose radio was blasting out reggae music which was not altogether unpleasant to Eddie's untrained ears. Eddie looked down at himself and discovered that the powers that be had dressed him suitably for the occasion. His old white tennis shorts and t-shirt felt familiar and comfortable. He would not look out of place if he became visible. Though he knew that the chances were very slim, if not infinitesimal, he still glanced about nervously when he got to his feet.

The young couple seemed to be asleep when Eddie wandered over. He was extremely curious as to see who they were and if he might recognise either of them. There had to be a reason for his arrival on what appeared to be such a lonely and isolated beach, he thought. Apart from the coloured man, there wasn't another soul in sight, although there did seem to be movement and noises coming from an old tin shack-cum-beach bar at the top of the long sandy beach.

The man and woman appeared to be in their early twenties and each had acquired a deep tan, their well-oiled bodies glistening in the strong sunshine. Both had wedding rings on the third finger of their left hands. They were married. As Eddie circled the young people, there wasn't much else his inquiring mind could determine about the strangers. The man had about a week-long growth of beard on his face which, perhaps, gave an indication of how long they had been on holiday, for holidaying sun-seekers they clearly were. Despite the vague disguise, Eddie was absolutely convinced that he had never seen the man before. At first, when he had approached the young couple, he had thought or hoped that they would be familiar, possibly even being close family, but if, as he suspected, it was later than 1969, then Jenny and Gary would have appeared slightly older. Close inspection of the recumbent couple had revealed them to be only just out of their teens. He wasn't, however, so sure of the girl and he began to study her more carefully, even dropping to his knees for a closer view.

"Are you doing anything tomorrow? … I was wondering if you'd like to go to Hamsden to do some shopping and …."

Eddie jerked his head upright and looked around himself. It was instantly clear that the voice had come from inside his head and it was familiar.

"… you've got my number, haven't you?"

The voice was more than just familiar now. Identical words to the ones he had just 'heard' had once been spoken to him on a Friday afternoon in late January of 1966. That day, he had been accompanied on his walk home by one Sally Barber, a fellow pupil in Fenton Grammar School's fourth year. Other snippets of a hurried conversation resurfaced.

"Oh good, you have decided to come, Eddie …."

Then he heard his own voice reply.

"Can't stop, Sally, I've got to go back home; I've forgotten something."

The girl began to stir and opened her eyes. Eddie jumped away and out of her eye line though there was no need as she had been immediately blinded by the sun. She rolled over onto her stomach, laid her head down once more and closed her eyes. A familiar movement, the shape of the eyes or just wishful thinking – whatever the reminder had been, Eddie knew that he was looking down at Sally Barber and, for the first time since his passing, his ghostly soul felt real emotion. He was looking at someone who could have become his first girlfriend when he had been fourteen. He had, however, made other plans for that late January Saturday with disastrous and fatal consequences. If only he had taken Sally's offer up of a trip to Hamsden for shopping and 'so on' – to use her words uttered on the walk home the previous day – *he* might have been the young man who was currently lying beside her on this faraway beach.

After a couple more minutes spent thinking about what might have been, Eddie wandered away with no particular plan in mind. Out of nothing more than idle curiosity, he made his way slowly over to the only other person in sight on the small secluded beach. For the first time he studied his surroundings. The beach was small; no more than three hundred yards wide and fifty deep and hemmed in by groves of palm trees that flowed right to the water's edge. Behind the beach was a narrow dirt track that wound its way up into densely forested hills. The small beach bar seemed to have no more than two or three customers and their only means of transport in and out seemed to be a couple of open-topped jeeps. At least one of the vehicles had markings on the side to indicate it belonged to some small boarding house further inland. There was no other sigh of human life or habitation – the little cove was clearly a closely guarded secret. From his scant knowledge of the music blaring from the tinny radio that lay next to the muscular coloured man, Eddie made a mental guess that the beach's location was somewhere in the Caribbean. The West Indian reached over and turned up the volume.

'After she walks away
Then sadness comes
And without your love
Then you'll find out how
Hard it is to be alone'

Eddie caught this verse in its entirety as he stood beside the young man who, by then, was sitting up and singing along to the words, greatly helping Eddie with the translation from the West Indian dialect into something approaching English. The young man looked sad as if the lyrics of the song had some personal significance. In the background and behind him, Eddie could hear an argument start up between Sally and her husband.

"… *I didn't go to her room last night, Sal, honestly.*"

"*So where were you until two-thirty? Solomon said he closed the bar at one.*"

"*A walk, I told you, just a walk.*"

"*Where?*"

"*Anywhere – what does ….?*"

Eddie wandered back as the argument was getting more and more heated. Sally's husband obviously could not account for about an hour the previous night and Sally suspected the worse. By the time Eddie reached the couple, Sally had got up and, flouncing her way back up to the small shack, she managed to persuade another young white man to drive one of the jeeps. They sped away up the hillside in a cloud of dust; presumably back to wherever she and her husband were staying. Meanwhile, Sally's husband had assumed a sitting position with hands clasped round his knees, staring blindly out to sea.

'Then sadness comes …

… to be alone.'

Eddie felt sad for Sally. *He* would never have done anything like her husband was being accused of – Sally was too nice. Suddenly, he felt alone, too. Oh, how life can be so cruel, he thought. He wandered up the beach hoping that Sally would be happy for the rest of her life and would find true companionship.

The *Pineapple Cove Beach Bar* beckoned Eddie as he thought of his own loneliness at that moment. Being a ghost was fun most of the time, when there were things to do or people to annoy, but here on this isolated beach, at least two other people had cast a shadow over his visit back to the living world. Eddie felt the need for the sound of happy voices as he climbed, unnoticed, onto one of the cane bar stools. There were three other such seats, only one of which was occupied by a small Asian looking man of about thirty. The owner, Carlos by name, and clearly Latin by descent, sat opposite him behind the low bar. Both men were drinking what looked to be some kind of coconut punch, laced, no doubt, with rum. Dried pineapples hung on strings from the bar's wooden ceiling – giving any tourists a feeling of authenticity to the place. One minute after Eddie had taken up his position at the bar, the only other tourist, apart from Eddie himself, came and sat between him and the Asian man. Sally's husband was in need of a drink.

"A cold beer, Carlos, please."

"Yes, sir, Mr John. Comin' right up."

Carlos had a strange accent, a combination of Spanish and native Jamaican. Cards for taxis and restaurants, which lay scattered on the bar top, indicated that Eddie had indeed landed in the 'yard'. John nodded to his fellow drinker.

"Alright, Mo? How's business?"

"Not bad, John. When are you and the missus going back home?"

"Got another four days yet, but to tell you the truth, I'm ready to go now. I'd rather be back fighting fires than fighting Sal."

"You been up to no good again, then?"

"No, Mo – just because she saw me talking to another girl back at the hotel last night, she thinks I must have slept with her or something."

Carlos brought John his drink and interrupted the conversation.

"And did you, Mr John?"

John took a long swig of beer straight from the bottle and replied,

"Did I what?"

"Sleep with her."

"Oh, not you and all – of course I didn't. We just had some innocent fun; kissing and snogging, you know."

Carlos winked and said,

"I say nothing, Mr John."

"Well," continued Sally's husband. "You've got to have a bit of fun now and again, especially on holiday. She'll come round, she always does – loves being married to a fireman."

John finished his beer and ordered another. Eddie was simultaneously appalled and curious. How could anyone treat his wife like that, particularly one as nice as Sally? John seemed a thoroughly nasty piece of work. Eddie's curiosity stemmed from the mention of John's occupation. Did he work with Gary in Hamsden or had Sally moved away from the area before she had met him? Eddie had also been thinking about what time zone he had moved to after his and Len's journey to the moon which had been July 1969. Was he still in 1969? He tried to do some mental calculations. Sally had been about fifteen in early 1966 and she'd looked about twenty or twenty-one on the beach although, with her skimpy bikini, it was difficult to tell exactly. It was therefore, he decided, probably at least 1970.

While these questions had been going through Eddie's head, Mo, which turned out to be short for Mohammed, was trying his best to reprimand his fellow drinker.

"You shouldn't do naughty things, John. Your wife seems to be a lovely person. Don't mistreat her. You'll lose her, you hear?"

Mo's accent was pure Jamaican, despite his Asian ancestry. Eddie's ears pricked up at John's reply.

"I know, Mo. My mate Gary in the fire brigade back home lost his wife. Upped and took their two-month-old baby and went back to her parents."

"Why?"

"She caught him with some lipstick on his shirt collar. He'd been calling in on an old girlfriend on his way home some nights and word got around the station. Someone told his wife and, bingo, that was that."

By this time Eddie was getting quite upset within himself; the bar on having emotions as a ghost was being lifted for the second time that day. The timings all seemed to fit. Jenny and Gary got married in September 1968. It was quite possible, therefore, for them to have at least a baby of that age. If only he could ask John for the full story. John's third beer loosened his tongue still further.

"Yeah and he regrets his mistake – lovely girl she was. Lost her brother when he was fourteen, so she's had a bit of a rough life one way or another, you could say."

"Accident?" asked Carlos, joining in the conversation again after providing John with his fourth bottle.

"What?" said John.

"I said, did her brother die in an accident?"

"Oh, no – he just went missing one day. Never found a body. He maybe still alive somewhere, I suppose, but not very likely since it's been over four years now."

So that was it, thought Eddie, 1966 plus four years and a bit would make it the summer of the first year of the new decade, 1970. Also, he had been brought to the isolated beach just to find out, by chance, that Gary and his sister had split up after having a child and that he was an uncle. For one brief moment he wished he'd stayed in the oblivion of death. Real life was so cruel and hard, full of pain and regrets. Real life could be hell on earth. Why couldn't things just be good and straightforward for everyone? There were a lot of bad people about in real life, he concluded. It was much better to be dead where, at least, you couldn't get hurt, or into trouble, or lose your husband, and you certainly couldn't get ill or die. He and Len had already crossed man's biggest hurdle. Poor old Jenny – she didn't deserve this.

After a few more minutes, Eddie had had enough of listening to John, Mo and Carlos exchange views about the female race. 'Mr John' was getting fairly drunk, with his temporary companions doing their best to restrain him, but Carlos' profits were down and he'd quickly got him on to more exotic and expensive drinks. Just as Eddie jumped lightly off his stool, the driver of the jeep returned – he seemed to be employed by John and Sally's small hotel whose name was emblazoned on the jeep's sides. *Bay View Hotel* must be some way up into the hills, thought Eddie, judging by how long it had taken the driver to get there and back. Leaving the driver to join the other two men, Eddie set off up the dirt track to investigate. He thought he might be able to see how Sally was before the hotel jeep was once again employed to bring her husband back up to their accommodation. His own feeling of loneliness had receded – the day seemed to be designed for him and him alone and he was not missing Len much at all.

The walk-cum-climb would have been difficult for even the fittest of people, but Eddie, as usual, found it easy to glide along, sometimes taking giant strides on his journey up into the wooded hills. In less time than it had taken the jeep driver to get to the hotel and back, Eddie came in sight of the low, white-painted, two-storey building whose veranda seemed to enclose all four sides of the modest looking brick and wood structure. It seemed to be out of place in its grounds that had obviously been reclaimed from the natural forest that enclosed it. Once through the final trees, Eddie could see that the Bay View Hotel had seen better days but, on entering the foyer, he also noticed how clean and tidy everywhere was. It looked to be simply but adequately furnished for its guests who would, in any case, spend very little time there during the hours of daylight. To the right of the main foyer, the long bar looked inviting to thirsty and hot customers, but only the occasional rainstorm would probably attract most people to be there during the day. It was empty when Eddie looked in. He returned to the foyer and wandered over to the long low table that constituted reception. It was unattended, which mattered not to Eddie as he didn't possess the power of human speech in order to inquire which room Sally was in. He did, however, notice a calendar hung at an angle on the wall behind the table. The year, 1970, agreed with his earlier surmise but the date did not. It was, according to the page displayed, Friday, February the 13th. The scary associations of the date were bad enough for Eddie but to find also it was winter seemed even odder. Not being able to feel the difference between heat and cold, Eddie had assumed by the dress of the people on the beach, that it was summer. Little did he realise that day temperatures in Jamaica in February averaged out at 82 degrees and night ones at 72, with little or no rain all month. Winter in Jamaica was really a continuation of summer, just a little drier.

Eddie was at a loss as to what to do next – there didn't appear to be a key rack behind the table and, though it contained several drawers, Eddie had no physical way of opening them and his mind power, such as it was, failed to reveal their secrets as well. After a while he decided to investigate the hotel without directions. He soon discovered that the long front of the building was not reciprocated by its depth as he soon found himself in a large inner rectangular courtyard which was surrounded on all sides by about forty cabins. The second floor was galleried in an old colonial style but with less cabins leading off it, seeming to consist only of larger and more luxurious rooms and suites. The gallery was fit for purpose, as getting cool breezes to flow through the rooms had been essential in the hotel's construction. Eddie estimated that, in total, there were more than fifty rooms and suites to check if he was to find Sally. Glancing back down and around him, Eddie could quickly see that the courtyard was empty, except for a solitary gardener tending to various potted plants and shrubs which looked in dire need of water.

In room 33, on the north side of the ground floor, Sally Barber was alternating between sobbing and muttering oaths, both under her breath and out loud. In the end she only had one thought on her mind.

"Oh, I want to go home!" she cried to the ceiling. "I hate him, I hate him. Oh how I hate him!"

She then cursed her husband vehemently with words that she hardly was aware were part of her vocabulary and, with one final scream of frustration, she threw herself back onto the bed and buried her face in the covers.

Outside, Eddie heard her final shouting as he passed the first room on the north side, number 31. He skipped the last few yards and was soon outside number 33. If Len had been with him he would have boldly walked straight through the door, open or not. Eddie paused outside for a moment while he listened again. The shouting and screaming had been reduced to low sobs which soon subsided completely. Eddie made ready for the pass through the door of number 33. Somewhat to his surprise his progress was halted the moment his body reached the door and, try as he might, his newly acquired skill seemed to be no use. He took a pace backwards and tried the secondary method of concentrating his mind on the door. To begin with nothing happened; the door was proving difficult to crack. He tried again and this time the door creaked open a couple of inches but not wide enough to squeeze through if it was to continue to thwart his progress.

Inside room 33, Sally was just drifting off to sleep when the noise of her bedroom door opening caused her to wake with a start.

"John? Is that you? Go away and leave me alone."

When John didn't enter the room, she got up and pushed the door shut and locked it with the key – she was sure that she had done that when she'd first got back. She returned to the bed with a sigh. He wouldn't be able to get in now, she thought.

Eddie watched as the door closed and then he heard the bolt slide home. He tried again and this time he imagined himself inside the room, even though he'd never been inside it. Fortunately, he had a rough idea of the layout of the room – a cleaner had been working in room 17 when he'd walked by and he'd stolen a peep inside. He heard the bolt slide back and this time the door opened almost halfway. Before Sally had a chance even to get up off her bed, Eddie slid easily into room 33. He turned round as soon as he got inside to see Sally putting her weight against the door and cursing it under her breath. She turned the key in the lock, took an upright chair from a corner of the room and wedged the top of its back under the door handle. With that, she fell back onto the bed. Almost as many curses had been directed at the door as had been directed at her absent husband earlier. Exhausted, she rolled over onto her side and closed her eyes.

Fortunately for Eddie's tender years, she had put on shorts and a top to cover her tiny bikini. Had she not done so, thoughts of what might have laid in store for him, if he'd lived, would have troubled him again. He seemed to have made up his mind what he was going to say to Sally, whether or not she was asleep.

"Sally, I don't know if you can hear me, but I hope some of what I say sinks in."

Eddie paused and seemed to gather himself.

"I'm really sorry that I didn't come to Hamsden with you that day. I realise now that I made a big mistake. All I can say is that I am happy where I am now and I'm having fun with my old friend Len, who, no doubt, you remember. I'm so sorry that you and your husband have had an argument, but I have to tell you that I don't think he's a very nice man and, even though he says he didn't go to her room last night, he did kiss and cuddle that girl. If you don't believe me just ask Carlos or Mo down at Pineapple Cove – he was bragging to them earlier."

Sally turned over onto her other side and gave a sleepy sigh. Eddie paused to see if she would wake and, when she didn't, he continued with his last message.

"And Sally, if I'd lived you would have been exactly the kind of girl I would have loved to have fallen in love with and married. I think you're gorgeous now and far too good for the likes of John. Don't stay with him, Sally – he'll only do it again. He doesn't respect you even though he thinks and says he loves you."

Sally moaned. Eddie blew her a kiss and this time, with his mission accomplished, the door did not provide a barrier to his exit and he was soon outside and crossing the courtyard. As he wandered back to the beach, waiting for his next return to darkness, Sally Barber left the Bay View Hotel in a taxi, with her suitcase aboard and bound for Kingston airport en route back to her mother in Fenton-on-Sea. She had tears in her eyes – tears that were not only because she knew her short marriage was at an end, but also for the memory of a fourteen-year-old boy she had once asked to go shopping in Hamsden with her on a Saturday in late January 1966. Her dreams had provided the catalyst for her decision to leave her husband.

John Richardson was very drunk. Already he had fallen off his stool on two occasions to be helped back onto it by Mo and Carlos. He was getting more and more voluble and angry.

"I'll show 'er when I get back. I'll show her who's boss, I will!"

"Of course you will, Mr John," said Carlos.

"You've had enough, my friend," added Mo.

"I'll let you know when I've 'ad enough. I can take my drink and anyone who says I can't is a …."

John's befuddled brain prevented him from thinking of an end to his sentence. The jeep driver, Wesley by name, came over and put his arm round the young Englishman.

"Come on, sir, I'll run you back up to the Bay View – sleep it off, eh? I expect young Miss Sally will be worried about you. I'm sure she didn't mean those things she said."

John threw back his shoulders to shake off Wesley's grip and promptly fell to the floor for the third time.

"Help him up, Wes," said the barman. "We'll get him in the jeep."

Carlos came round the bar and helped the driver with the drunken man. Fortunately, he did not put up a fight as the copious amounts of alcohol had at last deadened his senses and numbed his body beyond the point of physical resistance. By dragging and half carrying him, Carlos and Wesley, directed by Mo, eventually dumped Sally's husband unceremoniously in the back of the jeep. It would not be until the early hours of the following morning that he would wake up to find he was alone in room 33 where Mo and Wesley had left him.

Eddie barely noticed the jeep as it roared past him scattering dust and stones in all directions – he was too deep in thought to be bothered with his earthly surroundings. His visit to Sally's room had shown him another use for his new role and 'gifts' – they could be used to do good deeds and not just to have fun. He somehow knew that his advice had been received and understood by Sally – advice which, if given by a real fourteen-year-old, would certainly have been ignored. People might listen to ghostly guidance when all other earthly counsel had failed. The idea that God might use him to right wrongs or change things for the good filled him with some pride and anticipation for his next visit. He would have to tell Len when they next met, even though he might not be as receptive as himself. Just like in life, Len wanted to have fun. Philosophy was for other people far cleverer than him.

When Eddie got back to the beach bar, it seemed to be totally deserted; stools were stacked on the bar and glasses and bottles tidied away. The beach was empty, too, though in the distance Eddie could see a small dinghy about fifty yards off shore. Carlos was fishing for his dinner.

Eddie strolled down the beach to take a closer look. The barman seemed to be fishing with a simple bamboo cane and line which, judging by his excitement, meant that dinner was going to be lavish. For no apparent reason, other than for something to do, Eddie waved at the fisherman. To his shock and utter surprise, Carlos stood up in the small boat and waved back. Eddie nervously waved again and Carlos then shouted,

"Plenty of snappers for supper, Mo! How's our friend?"

"Sleeping it off, but Wes said that there was no sign of Sally."

Eddie's ghostly heart started 'beating' again as Mo walked past him from behind. Eddie breathed a sigh of relief – he'd had enough for one day without being visible to people as well. That was his last thought as night descended on his world again and he disappeared into oblivion.

9
Little Ed

By the end of the first year of the new decade, Jennifer Compton and her baby boy had been living back at number 38 Fir Tree Close for nearly a year. Even thought the Comptons had plenty of room for mother and son in their three-bedroom semi, tensions at times ran a little high. Eddie's sister had walked out on her husband, Gary, back in early January that year. Her husband's philandering had been the last straw in a year or so where Gary had not, by any stretch of the imagination, started married life in a sober and responsible fashion. As soon as their first child had been born, within fourteen months of the wedding, he had taken on a whole different attitude to Jenny and his new charge. He had already started to drink a lot almost immediately after returning from honeymoon, calling in at pubs on his way home from work. He seemed to regard the wedding as some kind of final piece in his relationship with Jenny and not as a confirmation of his love and care for her and the start of a new life, where give and take had to become a reality for them both. It certainly wasn't like that as far as Gary was to be concerned. He seemed to be the embodiment of male chauvinism in his total lack of responsibility with regard to his fatherly duties, when it came to nappy changing and feeding etc., or, indeed, even with day to day household chores. Jenny was often the recipient of remarks such as: '*I'm working and bringing the money in, so why should I do the …?*'

At first, Fred, and particularly, Ann Compton had welcomed their daughter and their grandson back with open arms. Jenny's dad had originally had some misgivings about Jenny's choice for a boyfriend when she had only been sixteen, but as he had come to know Gary, over time he had come to like and respect him. He was thus disappointed when the split became permanent. For her part, Ann Compton gained great enjoyment from having her daughter back and her grandson to play with and care for, too. But after nearly a year without Jenny working and able to contribute to household expenses, things had become a little tight financially and, not for the first time, Jenny's dad raised the issue at teatime on Wednesday, December the 30th. Fred Compton had returned to work after his short Christmas break only the day before.

"Here am I the only one working and you two sit at home all day, and little Eddie here has two mothers to look after him."

"Call him Ed or Edward, Fred. You know how I don't like Eddie," said his wife.

She then went on to say something about how much effort was required to look after a baby in the early months, but it seemed to have little effect on what her husband seemed determined to say.

"Surely, Jenny, you can at least go back part-time at Curls and Twirls. You said Mrs Winter said you could when you were ready. Isn't it about time now, given that Ed isn't waking you up much during the night and you won't be as tired as you have been?"

Fred seemed to mellow a little as her patted his daughter's hand.

"I know it's hard, love – I remember how your mum was with you and Eddie during the first year."

Jenny's mum suddenly seemed to be in agreement with her husband.

"I can look after little Ed during the day, love – your dad is right, we do need the money."

Jenny had said nothing while listening carefully to her parents and balancing Ed on her lap to feed him.

"Well?" said her dad. "What do you say, Jenny love?"

Jenny carefully lifted her son into his highchair and eventually replied,

"I just think that Gary should be paying you both to look after his son, Dad. Ed is his responsibility before he's yours."

Fred Compton sighed.

"And he will, believe you me, when you decide to get divorced. At the moment, unfortunately, you have taken custody of Ed and will have to look after him."

"He did send him some nice Christmas presents," said Jenny's mum in a conciliatory tone.

"Big deal, Mum!"

"Anyway," continued her dad. "Don't you think you need to get back to doing the things you like and are good at? You're a talented hair stylist now – everyone I know says so."

Her dad's persuasiveness and flattery began to make an impression.

"Well, if I did, I'd only want to do afternoons, Mum. Could you look after Ed then?"

Fred Compton smiled as his wife replied,

"Of course I could – it would be an absolute pleasure to spend some quality time with my grandson and, anyway, he sleeps a lot in the afternoons, Jenny."

"I know," said Jenny. "I just need to be here in the mornings."

And then she smiled and turned to her dad and said,

"Actually, Dad, I have been thinking about going back to work, but I didn't want you to think I was just going to dump Ed on you and Mum during the day."

"You silly girl," said her mum. "You wouldn't be dumping little Ed on me, love, and your dad is at work all day."

"Good, that's settled, then," said Jenny's dad.

Len and Eddie had not seen each other for nearly two 'years' when next their paths were to cross. The 21st of March 1971 was to be an unremarkable day for the human race; a day like any other day with no momentous achievements or events. It would have been, however, Eddie's twentieth birthday. It didn't seem like the first day of spring in Fenton-on-Sea when Eddie awoke from his year-long slumber. It had been a cold and frosty morning which, by his early afternoon arrival, had turned dank and drizzly. Again, his ears were the first to provide some indication of his exact location. This time, the almost complete absence of sound was to be more of a clue to those days of the week it couldn't be than those that it could. When his eyes eventually focused on his surroundings they confirmed quickly that it wasn't a weekday. Having found himself standing in the High Street and facing Woolworth's, Eddie could see by its unlit windows and absence of customers that it had to be a Sunday. Glancing up and down Fenton's main street completed his evaluation. He noticed he had been provided with his old duffle coat which covered some familiar warm clothes underneath.

"We've picked a good day to come back, haven't we, Captain?"

Almost unobserved, Len had appeared at Eddie's side and he didn't give his friend a chance to make a mistake this time as he continued with,

"Please tell me what the twentieth prime is?"

Eddie didn't bother to try any clever extra security checks and replied simply,

"Seventy-one, mate."

"Seventy-one it is, Eddie *old* boy," replied Len with added emphasis to 'old'.

"Less of the old, comrade!"

"Ah! Ah! And you don't know what the date is yet, then? Or do you?"

Eddie knew he was being challenged. He gave it his best shot.

"Judging by the shop displays across the road and the absence of shoppers, I would say it's a Sunday sometime around Easter and therefore in late March or Early April."

Len looked suitably impressed.

"Not bad, not bad. And the year?"

"Well," said Eddie as he cast his mind back to the date of his Caribbean interlude. "At least 1970, but probably 1971."

"Even better," said Len. "Now, what about the date? All I'll tell you is that it's a Sunday in March 1971."

Eddie walked around in a circle while he pondered Len's question. This was fun to have a puzzle over which to exercise his considerable mental ability. However, even his mathematical brain wouldn't allow him to do the necessary calculations to work out which days in March 1971 would be Sundays, even if he could remember any reference point to start from. Len expected him to get the answer so there had to be another clue. Len hadn't said much else since arriving except for implying he was old ….

"Got it, Len," said Eddie with a start.

"Well?"

"March the 21st – my birthday!"

"Well done, Captain! I knew you wouldn't let me down."

"How did *you* find out the date, Len?" asked Eddie.

"Usual trick. The newsagents on Steep Hill still had some of yesterday's papers in the window and, like you, I knew it had to be a Sunday."

By this time, and without discussion, the two boys had already started walking up the High Street. Eddie was curious as to what his friend had been doing since their incredible trip to the moon.

"So what happened to you on the moon, Len?"

"Don't know, mate. I can't remember much. Suddenly I was with you heading back to the lunar module and then it just went blank."

"What have you been up to since?"

"Nothing. After I disappeared into oblivion, the next thing I knew was finding myself at the bottom of Steep Hill about ten minutes ago. Anything in between is a complete blank. What happened to you after I left?"

"Not much more on the moon. I ran round in a panic looking for you, got back to the lunar module to find it locked and then, like you, I must have passed out. But I have been back to earth since – just over a year ago on February the 13th."

Eddie then spent the time it took the two ghosts to walk up to the entrance to Fir Tree Close to report back on his Caribbean adventure. Len was impressed but also added,

"I told you that you should have gone to Hamsden with Sally that day."

"Yeah, thanks for that. Hindsight is a wonderful thing, Len."

Len made no comment on Jenny and Gary's reported separation and he remained silent until they had reached number 38. It had been obvious to him from Eddie's story that his friend wanted to see how his sister was as soon as possible. The two boys paused for a moment outside the Compton's front gate.

"You didn't like Gary from the start, did you Eddie."

"No, I suppose not, but I had grown to like him and so had Mum and Dad. Like Sally and her husband, you just never know what's going to happen when a relationship is formalised by marriage."

"That's pretty deep, mate. You're only supposed to be fourteen, you know."

"You and I may still look fourteen but I'm beginning to discover that our minds and souls age with our natural years."

Len mumbled something about still feeling he was fourteen and didn't want to be twenty, to which his friend said,

"And I'm an uncle, Len."

"Uncle Eddie, eh? It has a nice ring to it," said Len. "Can you be an uncle at twenty?"

Eddie ignored a possible debate over his age and asked, rhetorically,

"I wonder if I've got a niece or a nephew"

"Only one way you're going to find out," replied Len. "That is, if your sister is still living here and we can get in."

Eddie nodded and walked through the closed gate. He would have to share his other thoughts with his friend at a later time. He would choose his moment to discuss the idea of using their extraordinary powers for good and not just for their own amusement.

Sunday lunch with the three generations of Comptons had been a longer affair than usual that Sunday. A lavish turkey roast had been followed by a dessert to die for and all accompanied with a bottle of good champagne, provided courtesy of Jenny's new wages. Fred and Ann always tried to celebrate on their late son's birthday in style and without tears. Eddie's mum said every year that the day had to be enjoyed by all and was not to be a time for sadness. Of course, on the previous five occasions someone had always disobeyed Ann Compton's rule and had eventually dissolved into a state of 'self-indulgent grief', as she would call it. By three o'clock, Fred Compton was on his second glass of whisky – he'd also managed two large glasses of bubbly with his lunch. Given that he'd also downed a couple of pints in the Red Lion after Sunday morning service at St Andrew's, he had just about reached his 'emotional' state that afternoon. It would be his turn to exhibit the self-indulgency. His wife, suspecting he had gone well beyond his normal limit for alcohol, had quietly repaired to the kitchen to wash the dishes and leave her daughter to cope with her husband's inevitable outpourings. Little Ed had toddled after his grandmother on chubby and still somewhat unsteady legs.

"He would have been in his second year at University now, you know, Jen."

"Yes I know, Dad. Do you think it would have been one of those posh ones?"

"What? Like Oxford or Cambridge? I don't know, love. Maybe we wouldn't have been able to afford it."

Jenny's dad drained his glass and reached for the bottle containing the 'water of life'.

"Dad, don't have anymore. You know Mum doesn't like you drinking too much."

"'s only once a year."

"No more after this one, then? Promise?"

"Y'p. I promis'."

"Dad, you're already slurring your words."

"No, I'm no'."

Jenny reached over the dining room table and picked up the bottle of good malt, screwed the top firmly back on and took it into the kitchen. She smiled at her mother and said,

"Get the bed ready; he's had too much, Mum."

By the time Jenny got back to the dining room, it appeared that her dad had been carrying on the conversation without her.

"… was the brightest boy at Fen'on Grammar. I said, he was the brightest boy at school, you know."

"Yes, Dad, I heard you," said Jenny as she sat down at the table.

The next five minutes were taken up with Jenny listening patiently while her dad lauded all his son's achievements, including some that hadn't even belonged to him. In the end, however, Fred Compton didn't cry, and when he saw his wife and grandson return from the kitchen, his normal sensible, serious and responsible nature took over and he agreed with his better half that he needed a couple of hours sleep. It had been a tiring week at work, he said!

After her father had gone upstairs, Jenny laid little Ed down for his afternoon nap in his cot in 'Uncle Eddie's' bedroom, as she called it. She then went back downstairs and joined her mum to watch a film on television.

Len kept himself a few feet behind his friend as they walked up the Compton's front path, more out of respect for Eddie than anything else – it was Eddie's family and not his own, which now consisted only of his mother, Mrs Martha Wilby in Kent. Len watched as his friend passed smoothly through the freshly painted front door. He waited a few seconds and then walked forward to follow Eddie but, as soon as his body got within a few inches of the door, some invisible barrier prevented him from doing so. He tried again several times but without success and, even when he tried to think his way in, nothing happened. In the end he realised that this visit was for Eddie and Eddie alone, and he wandered back down the path and out into the road. For the next ten minutes or so, he paced up and down to the end of Fir Tree Close, occasionally coming back to check on any happenings at number 38.

Meanwhile, his friend had found the house very quiet and, at first, Eddie thought that no one was at home. He looked in the kitchen, which seemed to indicate nothing; it was clean and tidy as usual. Approaching the far end of the hall, he at last heard the familiar sound of a television. It was just after four o'clock. Eddie hesitated nervously before trying to enter the lounge – he had heard no sounds of a baby crying and, so far, he had seen no other signs of one either. Although he hadn't observed the Sunday afternoon ritual in the Compton household for over five years, he did remember that his parents would never usually have been watching television at that time. He walked forward and listened. He thought he could hear other sounds above those emanating from the television – two female voices above the background noise. He metaphorically drew breath – he hadn't been in his old lounge for a very long time.

"*Have you seen much of Gary, Jenny?*"

"*No, not much, Mum – last time was before Christmas in Hamsden when I went for my lunch with Jean one day at Pritchard's.*"

Eddie entered the room and the very first thing he noticed was a large framed photograph of himself, hanging in obvious pride of place over the mantelpiece. It looked like one taken at Fenton Grammar when he had been in the third year. The next thing was the two women, both of whom were sitting side by side on the settee. Jenny was reading a fashion magazine and his mother was knitting – nothing much different here, then, thought Eddie. He glided over to his old armchair and sat down. The rest of the room seemed much as he remembered it, except for a fresh lick of paint and a few extra photographs of mother and baby. Closer inspection could not reveal whether the baby was a boy or girl. There were no wedding snaps to be seen anywhere. Eddie listened to the conversation, with one nagging thought in his mind. Where was his dad?

"He was with a girl, Mum."

"Did that upset you?"

"No. It would have done a year ago, but it only confirms that I made the right decision."

Eddie's mum stopped knitting.

"You did love him though, didn't you, Jenny?"

"Yes, I loved him with all my heart and soul, but sometimes I think I loved him too much, Mum."

"Too much?"

"Yes, Mum, no one can be that perfect. I'd put him on a pedestal from the day I first went out with him when I was sixteen. I saw in him what I wanted to see – I loved the Gary of my dreams. I ignored some warning signs early on – I was looking through rose-tinted spectacles."

It was obvious to Eddie that this was probably the first time that mother and daughter had actually shared their thoughts on what had led up to Jenny's separation from Gary. Both seemed to have tears in their eyes and Jenny's mum relieved the tension by saying,

"Let's have a nice cup of tea and try to put the past behind us."

"I have, Mum, and I'll have a coffee, please."

Jenny's mum left the room and it gave Eddie a chance to study his sister more closely. Though she looked older – she had to be twenty-four by then, he thought – motherhood had enhanced her beauty. She'd let her blond hair grow below shoulder length and though her eyes bore some emotional scars, overall she had grown into a lovely young woman. Eddie also noticed that she had let her natural cheek and eye colours come through; much less 'paint' was evident. Hearing the lounge door open, he moved away from his sister as his mother returned from the kitchen carrying the drinks.

"Here we are, love, just as you like it with cream."

She then put her own cup of tea down and said,

"I'll just go and check on your father – he had far too much to drink lunchtime."

"O.K., Mum. Will you look in on little Ed for me. He might be waking soon."

"Yes, love."

Eddie's face formed into a proud grin. His little nephew was called Ed, then. Also, and almost more importantly, his dad *was* here and not ….

"Jenny named him after me," he said out loud.

Soon, Ann Compton returned to the lounge to be with her daughter.

"They're both fine, Jenny," she said as she sat down beside her.

Eddie had spent the few minutes while his mum had been upstairs with a warm glow inside him and it was about to get warmer. Since it was clear to Eddie that mother and daughter were going to spend the rest of the afternoon in a comforting and sleepy silence, he made his way out of the lounge to explore upstairs. His dad had obviously overdone it earlier but his main and immediate desire was to see his baby namesake.

Eddie guessed where little Ed would be and, with the door half open, he was able to squeeze into his old bedroom without any ghostly trickery. Baby Ed was awake and standing up with his hands on the top of the cot side. He was smiling. Apart from the nice surprise that his nephew had suddenly woken, the first thing Eddie noticed was the baby's colouring. Though it was still very short, his hair had a gorgeous ginger tint and his face possessed that freckly quality similar to his own. He really was a little Eddie. His older namesake couldn't prevent himself from saying something in his silent world.

"Hello, little Ed. I'm your Uncle Eddie."

What happened next would haunt Eddie for some time to come, even though he knew that such a haunting was ridiculous. Spontaneously, as Eddie spoke his words of introduction, little Ed reached out both his arms to his uncle and gave an excited smile which said: '*Pick me up, Uncle Eddie*'. Uncle Eddie took a step backwards but little Ed's face took on an even more beseeching look and his chubby little fingers opened and closed in a gesture of desperate pleading. 'This can not be happening', thought Eddie. 'I must be dreaming it'. He quickly moved his position, but the little boy's eyes seemed to follow him round the room until, when Eddie had squeezed himself into a corner of the room, little Ed climbed round the sides of his cot in order to be as near as he could to his uncle. Whatever emotions Eddie experienced at that moment, given that his ghostly body didn't usually exhibit any, the strongest one that enveloped him was fear – he was downright scared. He backed himself along the bedroom wall until once again he squeezed himself through the half open door and out onto the landing. Immediately, little Ed gave a screech of frustration and burst into tears. Eddie didn't wait to see if matters got even worse and the little boy suddenly said something. At that precise moment, his mind would have interpreted any incomprehensible baby groan or gurgle as sounding exactly like his name.

Downstairs, mother and daughter heard the baby crying.

"He's awake, Mum. I'll go up," said Jenny.

Her mother offered no response – the exhaustions of the day had taken her to the land of sleep and upstairs, her husband had, at that precise moment, exited the same place with the comforting words,

"Now then, little fellow, don't cry."

Fred Compton was awake and heading for the baby's bedroom. His son was halfway down stairs when Jenny 'brushed' past him.

"I'll get him, Dad. You go and have a wash and tidy yourself up. You'll scare little Ed looking like that"

Jenny's dad looked awful – hair all over the place, sweaty face and reddish eyes. After Jenny had eventually brought little Ed downstairs, it would be several minutes before she would be able to pacify him. Her mother would blame Jenny's father for looking in on him in such a 'wild man' state, as she would say.

Eddie didn't stop until he had made the passage through his parent's front door and down the path to the road. Len was on one of his many walks back from the end of the Close. Spotting Eddie from a distance, he ran down the middle of the road to greet his friend.

"Well, is it a boy or a girl?"

"A boy," said Eddie curtly and without further comment.

"What's up, mate? You look awful. You should see your face – it's ghostly white."

Len laughed at his own joke, but Eddie didn't smile. He had started to walk quickly again as though he was trying to put as much distance between himself and his nephew. Len caught up with him as he turned into South Road.

"Slow down, mate. What's happened? Has someone …?"

Eddie eased his walk to an amble and said,

"No, no one's died, if that's what you thought."

"I don't know what to think, Eddie. You'll have to tell me. What is it? What on earth's wrong?"

Eddie stopped walking altogether.

"You won't believe me, I just know you won't."

"Believe what? You're annoying and frightening me now."

And then Eddie told him. After his slightly garbled story, Len asked,

"You mean he could see you?"

"Well, I am a ghost, Len."

"But you think he knew who you were, as well?"

"I don't know, but he wasn't afraid of me – he wanted me to pick him up and hold him. He wouldn't have done that if I was a complete stranger, would he?"

"But you are a complete stranger, Captain. He's never seen you before."

"He might have done."

"Oh yeah. How?"

"There was a large framed photo of me, taken when I was about thirteen, hanging on the wall above the fireplace."

"And you mean he recognised you from that? Sounds a bit far-fetched to me."

"Well how else could he know me?"

"I don't know. Maybe you just saw what you wanted to see. You wanted him to like you, I mean. Perhaps he's just a very friendly little boy who puts on a cute performance for anyone, if he wants to get his own way. You know what some kids are like."

"I suppose so, but whatever the reason, Len, he could definitely see me. I suppose I shouldn't be that surprised as, like I said, I am a ghost."

"We both are," said Len. "Little Ed's first encounter with the paranormal, eh? Hope he hasn't been scarred for life by your visit."

At last Eddie seemed to cheer up and he said,

"My sister looked beautiful, Len, and she seemed happy without Gary. She's back at work at 'Curls and Twirls', I think."

"What about your mum and dad?"

126

"Their fine, except Dad must have had too much to drink at lunchtime and had been packed off to bed. When I was there, I suspected that they'd had a mild celebration, it being my birthday today."

"That's nice, Eddie – better than being sad and miserable."

Len paused and then said, almost with wistfully,

"I wonder what Mum does on my birthday? In fact, I wonder what she does on any day during the year."

"Haven't you been back, then?"

"Not since the time just after I died and when you were still alive, Eddie. Remember, we don't come back very often, do we?"

"True. You would like to see her again, wouldn't you, though?"

"I think so – I'd like to sometime. The only problem is that Kent's a long way from the places I keep ending up. Here or America, for example."

"Maybe you've got to want to go back and see her. As soon as I found out about Jenny's marriage break-up, I wanted to go and see her, and here I am. It just happened for me."

"Would you come with me?"

"Yes, of course, but I'm not in charge. Perhaps a little prayer to the powers that be might help, no?"

"I'm not sure I would know how to pray. Never really been keen on things like that, Eddie."

Eddie grinned sarcastically at his friend.

"Really, and you a ghost, as well. You do believe in an afterlife, don't you?"

"I-I don't know," stammered Len.

"For goodness sake, Len. What do you think you're doing now?"

At last, Len grasped Eddie's point. He went into an awkward silence as, suddenly, Eddie's view of the world around him started to get blurred. Len watched as his view of Eddie also became hazy. It had been a long and mentally tiring experience for his friend. Within seconds, Eddie had vanished to return to a period of inanimate rest. After a few more minutes while he thought about his own mother down in Kent, Len followed likewise.

10

A Familiar Jaunt

Eddie was to emerge again from his restful void much sooner than on previous occasions – less than three weeks had passed, measured in earth terms, when he awoke to bright sunlight. He found himself in a standing position and facing a familiar view. With the Cork Lightship to his left, the pier to his right and a bright blue sea in between, he was nowhere else but in his hometown of Fenton-on-Sea. Eddie shook himself down and looked uncertainly behind him. It plainly wasn't a weekday this time, judging by the number of people promenading in the sunshine and it probably wasn't God's day of rest either – the pier's amusements were clearly open for business. It had to be a Saturday, and the height of the sun, coupled with the abundance of early spring flowers in the tubs on the promenade, pointed to April as the most likely month. Eddie began to wander back up the beach to see if he could determine anything more about his new arrival.

Len was waiting for him on the promenade, squeezed tightly and incongruously between two elderly ladies on a wooden bench. Eddie didn't forget the security check and was pleasantly surprised when Len responded promptly with the correct answer. Walking up the beach, he had been half-expecting Len's bad ghost to appear as it had been some time since it had presented itself on any new arrival.

"Good morning, comrade Len," said Eddie cheerfully.

"Good morning, Captain Compton, and a beautiful spring morning it is, too."

"I guessed it was spring and a Saturday as well, I should think."

"Is it? You have me at a disadvantage this time, mate. I've literally just arrived. Saw you down on the beach and found myself between these old dears. Recognise either of them?"

Eddie studied the two ladies, both patently beyond their God-given allotted time span.

"No, mate. Should I?"

Len stood up and, turning to face the old women, he said,

"Look at the one on the left. Some years ago you used to sit in a room with her for four or five hours everyday."

Eddie walked closer and looked into the lady's face.

"Well?"

"Oh yeah, it's my old teacher at Fenton Central Junior School, Miss Wise," exclaimed Eddie. "She liked me – thought I was good at arithmetic. I finished all the books she gave me. In the end she had to make up worksheets just for me."

"Correct," said Len. "Don't know the other one, though. Do you?"

Eddie shook his head and said,

"No, but she might be her sister. They look alike."

The two Miss Wises' got uneasily to their feet, and arm in arm, they walked slowly away down the promenade. The boys replaced them on the seat.

"Well?" queried Eddie. "Why do you think we're here and when is it?"

Len had been counting as St Andrew's Church clock had been sounding the hour.

"Eleven o'clock, mate," he said. "Looks like spring but apart from that, I couldn't be more specific. No doubt, you'll tell me. As to the why, I have no idea."

Eddie gave his opinion.

"I think it's a Saturday in April and maybe still 1971. It doesn't feel much different to last time. We'll go up town in a minute and find out some way or other."

Eddie paused and gazed at his friend as he suddenly recalled their conversation on the last occasion they'd been in the living world.

"Don't you want to go and see your mum, Len?"

"I did try praying, but if God wanted me to go there, I think, I would have landed there instead of here. Besides, I don't think I'm ready yet."

"O.K., so what are we here for?" asked Eddie.

"Maybe for just for a bit of fun. Our lives shouldn't only be tied up with the past or trying to help people. We don't have responsibilities, do we?"

"True," agreed Eddie. "Perhaps God will have a mission for us on a later visit."

"You and your missions. Let's just enjoy ourselves, mate."

"Right," said Eddie. "That's enough waffling and discussion; so, where do we go? What do you fancy doing?"

"Another ghosts' day out," replied Len.

"Where?"

"Let's wander up the town and first of all determine what the date is – then we can decide."

"O.K., but on one condition," said Eddie.

"What?"

"We don't use any of our powers to get where we're going to go – no thinking our way there. I don't want to risk being separated from you. We both go together and by normal human means as well. It will be much more fun – no tickets to buy and we can get on any form of public transport without being seen or heard.

"Agreed," replied Len. "And we could slip into the odd Rolls Royce as well. I've always fancied being driven in a Rolls."

Eddie grinned. This day was going to be fun, he thought.

Inevitably, there seemed to be only one obvious place for the boys to head for initially that morning as a starting point for their day out. Fenton-on-Sea railway station was still, despite Dr Beeching's axe that had been wielded a few years previously, the quickest and most efficient way to exit the quiet seaside backwater. Eddie had also always been reminded by his father that the railways were the safest means of transport, public or private. On the way up the High Street, it didn't take them long to realise that it was Easter Saturday – the shop window displays, and the many people carrying Easter eggs, confirmed the date. In addition, the year was indeed 1971 as Len was able to verify from newspapers on a stand outside the main station entrance, above which the clock read eleven thirty-five on their arrival. Inside the station forecourt, they paused to debate their ultimate destination.

"Your choice, Len," said Eddie.

"Yeah, but we must both want to go there, right?"

"O.K., but we have to go to Hamsden first – we can't get anywhere else until we do."

"Obviously."

Len's knowledge of the geography of the United Kingdom was not as wide or as detailed as his friend's and he spent some time in deep thought.

"Come on, Len, make a suggestion," urged Eddie.

"Well, not London – we've been there for some fun," replied his friend. Then Len's face lit up.

"I know, Eddie. What about somewhere we've both been before on holiday?"

Eddie was pleased that Len was about to suggest the one place in England that he also wanted to go to, but had been reluctant to mention it first in case Len didn't agree.

"Where?" said Eddie, coyly.

"Devon."

Eddie milked the moment.

"Devon? Why Devon?"

"Because that's where we …."

Len stopped speaking as he spotted Eddie's ironic grin get even wider. When the penny dropped, he said,

"You knew where I meant all along, you clown!"

"Yes, and, remarkably, that's where I would like to go to, too."

Ludmouth, a small seaside town on the south Devon coast, was the place where Eddie's parents had taken him and his friend on two consecutive summer holidays when they had been twelve and thirteen. It had been in Ludmouth, too, where they had first had encounters with a friendly ghost, culminating in a near-death experience with a diesel shunting engine. Both boys had clearly realised that they could now go back in their new ghostly roles, and not just as ordinary living tourists. As he would remind Len later, Eddie had also been on an additional and solo excursion to Ludmouth, in mysterious and fantastic circumstances during the year before he died.

The boys made for Platform One to wait for the Hamsden train which ran every half an hour on a Saturday. Len confirmed the day's precise date on the sign hanging above the platform.

"April the 10th, Captain, sir."

"So that makes it a quick return visit to the land of the living, comrade. That's less than three weeks since we were last here," replied Eddie.

"Who's counting?" said Len with a shrug of his shoulders. "We're still fourteen by the look of it, though I'm beginning to think we need some new clothes. It won't be long before we'll look out of place."

For the first time that morning, Eddie studied his clothes in detail. Again he found he had been dressed in a familiar, but definitely ageing, pullover and pair of trousers whilst his friend, though similarly attired, had a light cotton jacket for extra warmth – England in April could still be chilly.

"I could do with one of those," observed Eddie.

"I think you could arrange that for yourself," replied Len slyly. "We just need to find you a nice trendy clothes shop and all you have to do is somehow persuade a jacket to land on your shoulders. A quick demonstration of your powers as a poltergeist should do the trick, literally!"

Len's suggestion didn't seem to sit too well with Eddie's ultra honest nature, but he had to agree it would be good fun to try the stunt. The vision of a jacket lifting itself of a rack and then moving smoothly out of the shop, apparently unsupported by anything tangible underneath, appealed to his scientific mind. That is, of course, if the jacket didn't become invisible, as he would be, when it joined its wearer. That would be a big disappointment, thought Eddie.

Though the 11.50 train was busy for the last shopping day before the Easter break, the two silent entities found seats in a middle carriage. But, as Len would continually observe: '*Who needs room when we can fit in anywhere?*' At least, in their present positions, facing each other across a carriage, they could see each other talking. Having passed Linham Junction, Len wanted to check the route that they were going to take beyond Hamsden.

"Do you remember how to get there, Captain?"

"More or less. We catch the London train from Platform Two, I think, and then get across London by underground to Waterloo for the train to Exeter, possibly changing at Salisbury. Once we get to Exeter, we change for the train down to Ludmouth Junction and walk the rest of the way."

"Or jump in BB's free hotel taxi."

"We probably won't be there in time and I bet it'll be long after dark when we get there, unless …."

"Unless? Unless what?"

"Unless we can get a faster train from London to Exeter. If you remember the route we went on with my mum and dad from Waterloo seemed to take ages. I seem to remember Dad saying that there was an express service from Paddington direct to Exeter."

"So, we go for that, then," said Len. "How long will it take altogether?"

Eddie muttered some mental calculations out loud and then said,

"It's still got to be at least five hours just to get to Exeter from the time we leave Hamsden, assuming there's a train that leaves around half past twelve and we can get across to Paddington in forty minutes, *and* there's a train leaving for Exeter within twenty when we get there."

"Half past five, then," said Len.

"Yes, plus the time from Exeter to Ludmouth Junction plus however long it takes from there to Ludmouth town."

"Worse possible case scenario?"

Eddie thought briefly and replied,

"Seven-thirty."

"Best case scenario?"

Eddie did some more calculations.

"Well, if we can cut the time to cross London to twenty minutes, and we're able to jump from one train to another each time within ten, and BB is there with his taxi, we could make it by just after six."

"We can do it, Eddie. Remember, on the underground we won't have any tickets to buy; we can glide quickly through queues and if we have to, we can hurl ourselves down escalators. And if a train is just about to leave when we arrive at a station, we can jump through the door of the one we're on; run and leap to another platform and jump into the next train, even if it's already started to move."

Eddie had to agree that they did have the powers to increase the speed of their journey, but he wasn't quite so sure that they should use all the ones his friend had described. However, with their train already pulling into Hamsden, they had no more time to discuss the problem or, indeed, what they were going to do when they got to Ludmouth if twilight was fading fast into night.

Exiting the train, Eddie shouted after his friend, who had leapt off first,

"Platform One! Platform One! There's a train there. Run!"

Less than a minute later both boys were sitting in an empty carriage waiting for the 12.25 express service to London Liverpool Street to leave. They were already ahead of Eddie's schedule by five minutes.

Apart from a worrying moment when Len seemed to dose off, causing Eddie to think for one moment that he was going to disappear, the journey to Liverpool Street was otherwise uneventful. The train arrived only two minutes late at four minutes past two. Following Len's earlier suggestions for crossing London quickly by tube, the two boys reached Paddington at twenty-one minutes past the hour – their time cushion had risen to six minutes. Unfortunately that was soon wiped out when they discovered that the next train to Exeter and Devon would not be until ten to three. With some time to kill, they headed for a row of station shops, one of which turned out to be selling, rather conveniently, a range of designer denim jackets and jeans. Eddie perused such labels as he could see until, after a few minutes, he thought he'd found a jacket that might fit him. He called his friend over to discuss the next step.

"So how do you reckon I can do this, Len?"

There were four or five other customers in the open-fronted shop and Len replied,

"You need to concentrate hard and try to imagine the jacket on your shoulders."

"What if the jacket starts to move and someone puts it back because they think they've knocked it off the rack?"

"We need a distraction, Eddie, I think. Let me see what I can do. You get ready for my signal and if it works, run like hell – O.K?"

Eddie nodded, fearful of what his friend might have in mind. Len sidled over to the other people in the shop. Once he had engineered a position that was roughly in the middle of them, he started his 'distraction'. A split second later all the lights in and just outside the shop went out, plunging the immediate area into semi-darkness. Simultaneously, a shelf of men's shirts deposited its wares amongst one or two of the customers. Despite the gloom, Eddie saw his friend raise his thumb at him. He closed his eyes and concentrated. Pandemonium had broken out at the back of the shop as the assistant tried the light switches and customers stumbled about, bumping into more racks of clothes and thus causing even more chaos. Len heard Eddie shout,

"Got it! Let's go!"

Len joined his fellow ghost outside the shop and grinned cheekily.

"Very nice, Captain, it goes with your role."

Eddie looked down at the grey denim RAF-style bomber jacket. He really did now feel like Captain Compton.

"Alright, Mr Navigator, get us to our transport, please."

Len led the way to Platform Six where the express to Exeter was waiting. Being Easter, it was heavily packed with families making a late getaway for the weekend. Eddie and Len found it more convenient to park themselves in the space near an exit door in the very front carriage. To begin with, Len placed himself on top of a pile of suitcases while Eddie stood opposite him surrounded by further luggage. Len was perched so high that, had he been composed of living flesh, his head would have almost touched the ceiling. His precarious position on top of a pile of four large cases would also not have been a stable one. An even stranger thing happened when they had just left Reading after about thirty minutes of their journey. Eddie was first to notice that a smartly dressed man of about thirty had suddenly appeared between them. Though there was no need, Eddie backed himself in a corner and then, realising what the man was going to do, said,

"Look out, Len, he wants his case."

The man reached up with both arms and pulled the top suitcase off the pile. Instinctively, Eddie reached out to stop his friend falling forward. Instead, as the man took his case away to find a more convenient position for it, Eddie was astonished to observe his friend remain stationary, suspended in his sitting position in mid-air! Len glanced down below himself.

"Oh, wow! That's a new trick, Captain – I can fly!"

"Be careful, Len," said Eddie with natural but unwarranted concern.

"I will, old boy."

Len folded his arms and struck the regal pose of a king on his throne. Eddie was still concerned for his friend's welfare.

"Can you move? Can you get down?"

"Don't know, mate. It doesn't feel any different from before and why should it? I wasn't actually sitting on the cases to begin with, was I?"

"Well, try."

Len tried to relax and he reached down with his hands, but with no physical leverage possible, he stayed exactly where he was.

"Whoops!" said Eddie. "You'll have to stay there now."

He then appeared to burst out laughing.

"Shall I pull the communication cord and get someone to come and help you?"

Even Len was getting anxious by now.

"Don't be funny, Eddie. Get me down. I don't feel right."

"Well, you got up there in the first place. You must be able to get down again. Try thinking your way down."

Len screwed up his face and concentrated. He looked to be in some kind of discomfort. Then his position got much worse.

"Nothing's happening, Eddie, and … I-I can't move at all now."

"What do you mean?"

Len seemed to have gone completely motionless. His words seemed to have to force themselves through his pursed lips.

"I can't even move my arms or legs now and my eyes …."

Eddie looked at his friend's face. Cold blue eyes stared back at him. Len tried to finish his sentence.

"My mouth won't …."

Eddie took a pace backwards. This is serious, he thought. His friend appeared to be in a state of suspended animation and was locked into a waking oblivion. Had he gone back to his 'resting' state, only while he was still visible to him? He tried to climb onto the cases but only seemed to pass through them and his friend. Soon, even Len's image began to fade and, within a matter of seconds, he vanished from Eddie's view.

Eddie began to pace up and down his cramped space between the piles of cases. What was he to do? Had Len really gone back to sleep? It could be days, weeks, or even years before he reappeared. Though there were some advantages for him if he were a free agent again, Eddie was worried that things had taken a new twist.

As Eddie was deep in thought, the well-dressed man suddenly returned with his case and Eddie watched as he returned it to the top of the pile. For no apparent reason, he set off to follow him as he made his way back to his seat. He hadn't gone more than a couple of paces when he heard a voice behind him.

"*Good day, Captain. How've you been?*"

Eddie's face lit up and he turned round to see his friend once again perched on top of the pile of luggage.

"What happened, Len? Did you feel anything?"

"Been asleep, son."

There seemed to be something different about his friend that Eddie couldn't quite put his finger on to begin with. Something *had* happened to him, though, and then, while Len sat grinning, almost insolently at him, he realised that his friend was wearing a different pullover and no jacket.

"You've changed, Len."

"Have I? Can't say I've noticed."

Len's replies had been curt and detached. Eddie knew what he had to ask next.

"Tell me, Len, what's the twentieth prime?"

"How the hell should I know, Ed?"

Eddie repeated his security question.

"The twentieth prime – what is it?"

"I've told you – I don't know, why should I?"

"Because, if you were Len's good ghost, you would know the answer straightaway. That's why."

The ghost gave a mocking smile.

"But I'm not, young Ed. I'm bad, really bad and I can do bad things, too. Just wait and see."

Eddie walked forward and confronted the evil ghost face to face. He then screamed as loud as his ghostly lungs would allow him to.

"Go away! Go away! Get thee behind me Satan!"

The ghost gave a derisory grin and said,

"Alright, I'll leave you for now, but I'll be back sometime. You can't get rid of me yet. Oh, no – not just yet."

The evil phantom vanished from sight. Eddie smiled and, 'patting himself on the back', said quietly,

"I beat him – I beat the devil."

Instantly, Len's ghost reappeared on the cases. He was dressed as he had been when they started their journey that morning. He seemed to have at least heard some of Eddie's conversation with his alter ego.

"And it's seventy-one, before you ask, Captain."

"Thank God for that," replied Eddie. "What on earth was that all about? I had to deal with your evil ghost, you know."

"Yes, I know and I think I know what happened too, Eddie, or, at least I can hazard a guess."

"What?"

"*I* think it was something to do with the fact that I was attached to the cases when I was sitting on them, and when that man removed the top one, I somehow lost contact, not only with my seat, but also with this world as well."

Eddie frowned and looked doubtful.

"But that would mean that every time we sat on something and someone took it away, we would be taken too."

"It's a possibility, isn't it? We might also disappear if we were leaning against something and our support was suddenly removed. We haven't been in a place where that's happened yet, have we? So, who knows?"

Eddie tried hard to remember any other occasion when either of their supports, whether they had been sitting or standing, had been removed suddenly. He had to admit he couldn't recall one such event.

"We'll just have to be careful from now on," he said at last.

"Yeah, but it's not likely to happen very often. As long as we sit or lean against immovable objects, no one can pull them away from us, can they?"

"Hope you're right, Len. That was quite scary when you went, to have you replaced by the very embodiment of evil – pure evil. He didn't even flinch when I called him Satan."

"Me too, Eddie, but to be on the safe side we should change the code. He presumably knows the question now," said Len.

The Exeter express thundered into a tunnel as Eddie nodded and said,

"He might go and learn all the first few prime numbers as well. It has to be a totally different question and answer."

Len suddenly had a brainwave as light flooded back into the carriage as well.

"I remember that we heard 'Buzz' Aldrin say something strange immediately after he followed Armstrong onto the moon's surface. Only we and the two astronauts could have heard it. Do you remember what he said to Neil Armstrong?"

Eddie did remember because it had been a whispered remark that Mission Control in Houston almost certainly didn't hear or, if they had, it surely would have been made public – it was so trivial given the historic nature of that moment.

"As I recall, he said, '*Monterey Jack or New Jersey Blue, then*?'"

"Well done! What a memory," said Len.

"I suppose it stuck because it was such a light-hearted thing for Aldrin to say after the seriously dangerous feat they'd just achieved. So, what will the question and answer be?"

"Easy," replied Len. "One of us asks what 'Buzz' Aldrin's first words were when he stepped onto the moon in 1969"

"Monterey Jack or New Jersey Blue, then?"

"Precisely."

11

Good Ghost, Bad Ghost

Bob Brewin had had a long day, driving guests from the station at
Ludmouth Junction to his and his wife's bed and breakfast on The
Esplanade in Ludmouth itself. Families often chose the Saturday of the
Easter weekend to start a week-long holiday in the quiet seaside town on
the South Devon coast. The station at Ludmouth had closed a few years
previously, and visiting holidaymakers who arrived by rail found that it
then became about a three mile trek from the station at Ludmouth
Junction to the town proper. Bob and his wife, Pat, ran a modest guest
house, *Summer Breeze*, on the seafront and BB's courtesy taxi service
was, short of walking, the only means of transport for new guests to get
from the Junction to their accommodation.

The last train from Exeter, that had passengers booked into
Summer Breeze that day, was due to arrive at Ludmouth Junction at six
twenty-five p.m. It would be BB's tenth pick-up since the first arrivals at
eleven that morning. He was tired but also pleased that he and Pat had a
full guest house for the forthcoming week. They'd even had to close
bookings at the end of February; such was the attraction of the quiet
Edwardian backwater where time seemed to have stood still since that era
of grace and gentility. Elderly couples loved the seaside town for the
nostalgia it generated for them, and, despite its lack of amusements,
Ludmouth was good for children of a certain age and temperament,
playing on the sandy beach and fossil-hunting being two of the more
traditional pastimes.

The Exeter train was late arriving – by over ten minutes in fact.
The only visible passengers to alight at the terminus were a middle-aged
couple by the name of Grayson. It clearly wasn't their first visit to BB's

B and B, as Bob Brewin seemed to recognise them immediately they emerged onto the station forecourt. He leapt from his old and battered twelve-seat mini-bus and hailed the new arrivals.

"Bert, Edie! Over here!"

"Hi Bob, good to see you," called back Bert Grayson. "Weather looks set fair."

BB took the couple's two suitcases and deposited them in the back of the mini-bus via the rear doors. Bert and Edie Grayson climbed in through the sliding door at the side. The two additional passengers had already followed the Grayson's luggage in through the back. Climbing over the cases, they took the two rearmost seats. It was twenty to seven and there was about an hour of daylight left. BB started the engine and steered the mini-bus out of the station for the ten minute drive to *Summer Breeze*.

"I've put you in the same room as last year; at the front on the first floor, just as you requested," said BB.

"Great," said Bert Grayson. "I bet you've been busy bees this weekend, haven't you?"

BB smiled tiredly at his guest's pun. He'd had to get used to them, given his own abbreviated nickname – he gave out enough of them himself as well.

"Pat does all the real work – I'm just her bumble, I mean, humble helper."

Eddie and Len cringed.

"Same old BB," whispered Len.

"He's a gem," replied Eddie and then he asked, "What are we going to do when we get to Ludmouth?"

"No idea, Captain – it'll be dark soon. I suppose we could do some real haunting; scare a few guests and make Summer Breeze into a tourist attraction, being haunted and all. Make BB and Pat loads of money."

The mini-bus and its four passengers had reached the outskirts of the main town by now as Eddie replied,

"What – all night?"

"Well, what do you suggest, then? We can't do much in the dark."

"Something will turn up, Len. It's bound to. We could always go to sleep."

"Where?"

"Anywhere – on a floor, in a chair, anywhere."

"Can we sleep and still remain conscious?" asked Len after some thought. "Whenever I've felt tired in the past, I've just disappeared back to oblivion and nothingness. We might not reappear for months or even years and then not together either. Bit of wasted journey, then, don't you agree?"

"Like I said, something will present itself. Let's not worry till we get there. We can go to the bar, legally, and listen to the conversations. Have a few laughs with the guests – maybe break a few glasses or spill a few drinks."

"Now you're talking," said Len, as BB pulled the mini-bus onto The Esplanade.

After an hour of twilight, in which they wandered along the promenade and up into the town, identifying old haunts and familiarising themselves again with what Ludmouth had to offer, Eddie and Len returned to *Summer Breeze* at eight o'clock. Pausing outside the guest house, Eddie glanced to his right at the shadowy shape of the Red Cliffs in the distance.

"I wonder if the rock tunnel is accessible again; it was blocked by rocks and boulders the last time we both came, but there was a narrow entrance from the beach when I came on my own just over five years ago."

"When you became invisible, eh?"

"Yes, Len, and I don't recall it to be a very pleasant experience either, given I was still alive then."

"Better now you've got no physical form, Captain," replied Len as they glided through the half-open door to the guest house. As they did so, Eddie's mind continued to dwell on his previous visit. He had always wondered, since his physical death, whether his invisibility that day had been an omen of his impending demise. He had been given half the attributes of a ghost while still a living and breathing being. Within a few short weeks, he had passed over to full membership of the exclusive club.

Len was clearly heading for the bar when Eddie caught up with him in the small foyer of *Summer Breeze*.

"Wait up, Len. Don't start any of your tricks without me."

"Tricks? What tricks, mate? I'm just going to relax and study our fellow guests. Sort a few likely candidates out."

"For what?"

"Don't know, yet."

The guest house private bar was relatively quiet – the small dining room on the other side of the foyer still seemed to be full and only one or two people had wandered in for an after-dinner drink. Len made for the empty window seat which was likely to be shunned by most of the guests; it had a hard wooden surface and was more for decoration than for comfort.

"This should be a good place to sit, Eddie. No one else will want to use it and try and sit on us."

The boys had a good view of the bar and the door leading to the foyer. A young couple, obviously in the early stages of a relationship, was perched on stools at the bar and the only other occupant, an elderly lady, reading a copy of The Times, was sitting in one of the few available easy chairs situated next to the window seat. Eddie could read the headlines on the front page of the lady's newspaper with ease, and it was clear to him that April the 10th 1971 didn't seem to be a particularly momentous day in the history of the world. The old lady muttered something under her breath as the middle sheets of the large and unmanageable newspaper suddenly released themselves from her grip and fell to the floor. She bent down to pick them up and, in so doing, knocked her gin and tonic off a side table. Again she cursed quietly, picking up her empty glass with one hand and her missing pages with the other. To add to her frustration, the rest of her newspaper slid off the arm of her chair to lay soaking in the remnants of her spilt drink. She really had had enough by now and, using the worst language her gentile nature would allow, she muttered loudly,

"Oh, botheration. What a wretched nuisance."

"Got her!" said Len unexpectedly.

Eddie turned to his friend and said,

"You've started already, haven't you?"

"Yes, I thought she needed livening up. She looked a bit too stuck-up for my liking."

By this time, BB had emerged from behind the bar and, with much fussing and flapping about, he managed to calm the lady down.

"I'll get you another drink, Miss Taverner – on the house and here, let me take your paper and sort it out for you."

"You can throw it away; it's ruined and, anyway, I've read most of it. You might just save me the crossword, though. I'm going up to my room, before it gets too crowded."

BB rescued the newspaper and the lady's empty glass and called after Miss Taverner,

"Don't you want another G and T?"

"You may bring it up to room number fourteen at once, please, Mr Brewin."

BB seemed to baulk at Miss Taverner's formality and self-important command.

"BB won't like being treated like that. He hates being called anything but BB," said Eddie. "It's a wonder he puts up with her – I think she must be a regular visitor. I'm sure there was a Miss Taverner staying here the last time I came."

"Well, we'll perhaps we'll pay her a visit later on given that she was kind enough to let us know which room she's in. A little trip to room fourteen at about two tomorrow morning might be a fun idea. No white sheets or anything, just one or two tricks with her curtains or the light switch, eh?"

"You really didn't like her, did you?" said Eddie. "We could give her a heart attack or something."

"I suppose you're right; maybe we should select another guest for a haunting – someone who is likely to be of a less nervous disposition."

For the next two hours or so, the two ghosts listened in on several conversations as the bar filled up with guests relaxing after their dinners or returning from walks on the seafront. They occasionally shifted their position to stand near couples or families and, just before eleven with the bar empty of families with children, Eddie suddenly became uneasy about one particular gentleman who was sitting by himself in the chair Miss Taverener had vacated earlier.

"I'm sure that old bloke over there seems to be watching us when we move, Len."

"What – that funny looking chap who came in about ten minutes ago?"

"Yes, the one who looks like a painter or one of those arty types."

Len turned to stare at the old man who, to his surprise, stared back at Len, instantly giving him a sharp nod of his head.

"I think you're right, Eddie – he *can* see us, and I think I know who he is."

Eddie looked blank.

"Who?"

"Oh, come on, Eddie – think. Who sat next to us at dinner the first time we came here?"

"You mean, Mr Manders."

"Yes, Mr Jacob Denham Manders, our friendly ghost and saviour when we nearly got run down by the shunting engine," said Len.

"That means only we can see him, then."

"Yes, unless there are some other ghosts in the bar."

The boys suspicions were quickly confirmed when a middle-aged man, who seemed to be the worse for drink, wandered over from the bar and plumped himself down on the old man's lap. Mr Manders raised himself gracefully into an upright position, his body passing through that of the seat's new occupant. Before either boy could move, he had glided out of the bar, his image fading quickly before he had reached the door. Though Len then ran right out onto The Esplanade to look for him, he found no trace of their friendly ghost who could take on disguises from an elegantly and flamboyantly dressed Victorian gentleman to a common unkempt tramp. It was a few minutes while Len completed his search before he returned to the bar, where he remarked to Eddie,

"No sign of him – looks like we have competition, mate."

"Maybe, but I somehow don't think Jacob Manders is the kind of ghost to just indulge in scaring people or having fun at their expense. If he does do anything, I would say it would be to help people who are in trouble. He saved our lives, remember?"

"True," replied Len, thoughtfully.

By this time all the remaining residents had left the bar to retire to their rooms for the night and, though he looked a little edgy, Len seemed anxious to have some more fun.

"Upstairs, I think," he said.

"Are you sure?" asked Eddie. "It seems a bit mean to me – upsetting people, especially if they're of a nervous disposition."

"Oh, what the heck – what harm can we do?" Len said with some insistence. It was quite clear to Eddie that Len was going to get his own way. He followed his friend out of the bar and upstairs. It was fast approaching midnight.

BB had taken a double gin and tonic to room fourteen a few hours earlier, and its effect had put Miss Taverner to sleep well before eleven. At precisely two minutes past bewitching hour, according to her small bedside alarm clock, the ceiling light came on. A few seconds later it went out and over the next minute or so the light flickered on and off repeatedly until eventually it disturbed Miss Taverner who awoke reluctantly. The light remained on for the time it took her to get out of bed to turn it off. It was extinguished a split second before her finger touched the switch, causing the light to come back on instantly. She pushed the switch again and the light flicked on and off. Miss Taverner was cross now, and she was just going to go and find BB, when the light went out for a final time. The room stayed dark for the next few minutes while the elderly lady settled back to return to sleep. Hardly had she closed her eyes, before her alarm clock fell with a clang to the floor. Pulling the light cord above her head, Miss Taverener cursed and reached down to return it to the bedside table. Immediately there was a rush of air as the heavy bedroom curtains were flung wide open, knocking a couple of ornaments on the window sill to the floor. Miss Taverner's anger had given way to fear bordering on terror by now, particularly when her bedroom was then plunged into darkness. She screamed and headed for the door only to find that, when she tried the handle, it was locked. She screamed again and, this time, loud enough to wake the dead. Less than a minute later, a dishevelled and barely-dressed BB arrived and, after a warning tap on Miss Taverner's door, he turned the handle and walked in to find his elderly guest sitting huddled on the floor in the middle of the room. Both lights were on and the curtains were fully closed with nothing else out of place.

Miss Taverner did not finish her night's sleep in room fourteen. Though all the guest's rooms were fully occupied, she slept the remainder of the night on a Put-u-up in a box room on the top floor. She checked out at eight in the morning without paying her bill. She would never return to *Summer Breeze* for any future breaks.

Eddie had not waited in room fourteen while Len had finished his cruel and thoughtless party tricks. He had left the room to return to the bar the moment Miss Taverner had screamed for the first time, remarking as he did so,

"I've had enough of this, Len. I'll see you in the bar when you've grown up. Be it on your conscience if she has a heart attack, or worse."

As Eddie sat in an easy chair in the bar, dimly lit only by some security lights, he pondered his friend's rejoinder to his final remark: *'Conscience? What conscience? We ghosts don't have consciences'*.

His thoughts were suddenly broken both by a piercing and glass-shattering scream from upstairs and a whispered but commanding voice from close by.

"Get out, Eddie! Get out now and run as fast as you can. I'll see you on the promenade."

The voice sounded familiar and certainly friendly. Immediately, Eddie realised his mistake. He leapt out of his chair and ran out of the guest house, gliding unchecked through the locked front door. He didn't stop until he had reached a bench on the promenade a good way from *Summer Breeze*.

"You didn't check his identity, did you? When Len came back from outside, you just assumed it was still his good ghost. His good one came to find me and when he couldn't, he disappeared like me. I can only presume he has gone back to his resting state."

Mr Jacob Manders had joined Eddie on the promenade bench and had a comforting smile on his aged face. Eddie said nothing. Was this Mr Mander's good ghost? Was the whole episode a double-bluff? Who could he trust? As if Jacob Manders could read Eddie's mind, he said,

"Trust me, Eddie; I am on your side. My evil side disappeared years ago. I'm much further down the road than you. I always wanted to be good like you. Eventually, my good side won the day and, hopefully, on a permanent basis, too. As for Len, I'm not so sure. He can be good, but he also seems to enjoy his evil side. He's got to control that, you know, if ...."

"If?"

"If he is to progress as a ghost."

Eddie had the distinct impression that Jacob wanted to say more but didn't think his young ghost was ready for what he had been about to say. Whatever it was, Eddie felt safe and confident that Jacob was a good ghost and he began to relax a little. This was getting to be interesting; he would have to be extra careful from then on. If ever his friend's good ghost went out of sight, for no matter how short a time, he would always have to repeat the security check when he came back. If only he could trust Len, he thought, it would be so much easier. But, as Jacob had just said, his friend had a lot to learn. Somehow sensing it was not going to be possible, Eddie turned to thank his friendly tramp, but Mr Jacob Manders had vanished from the bench next to him. Eddie followed suit in a few more seconds.

12

Free-Fall?

Len had no recollection of his final few minutes in Ludmouth. For his part, one moment he was chasing ghostly shadows on the seafront and the next, everything went dark and blank. The two boys had found themselves back on familiar ground – the forecourt of Hamsden railway station. It appeared to be autumn, judging by the falling leaves on the road outside. It was clear and sunny with a crisp feel to the air. The station was busy with commuters exiting the trains and making their way into town. The station clock read 09.05 hours.

"Did you not even sense something was wrong, or that your bad side had taken over?" was Eddie's opening question after the new security checks had been done and he had related to Len the events at BB's guest house after he had gone walk-about.

"No, not a thing," said Len, who had been clearly disturbed by Eddie's story of the events that had taken place after he had departed the land of the living. The two ghosts had taken up positions leaning against a high wall and well away from any passengers.

"I wouldn't have done those things, Eddie, you know I wouldn't. I might have thought about it, but only in fun. I hope Miss Taverner was alright."

"So do I," said Eddie. "So do I."

Eddie hadn't yet told his friend of Mr Mander's warning and Len seemed to sense there was something else.

"Did Mr Manders say anything more?"

"Yes, and it concerns you."

"Me? How?"

"He said that he thought you could be good, but that also you enjoyed being bad sometimes. He said ...."

"Enjoyed being bad?"

"Yes, and that you had to try and control the urge to do evil things."

Len looked very unhappy at his friend's remarks.

"It wasn't the real me when my bad ghost did those things you said I did in Miss Taverner's bedroom. You know me better than anybody – you don't think I'm evil, do you?"

"No, of course I don't and Mr Manders didn't say you were – just that to progress as a ghost, you should concentrate on doing good things and, I suppose, limit, or eliminate entirely, those times when having fun might cause grief for other people. Remember, Len, you had already earlier thought about annoying Miss Taverner in her room when she was asleep. Where there's the thought to do something evil, you're not far short of doing it for real, because in our new state we have to be careful even when we just think about things in case we make them happen. You can have as much fun as you like as long as you don't hurt anyone else physically, or mentally. I think that's what he meant. I need to be able to trust you as well and not have to continually check that it really is you."

"Same thing works the other way round, too, Eddie."

"How do you mean?"

"I mean that your bad side could take over one day and I meet your evil ghost."

"Yes, I know, and it's all down to trust and faith. We have to trust each other, Len. O.K?"

"Of course. I want to be good and I'm not a bad person. I just don't think sometimes, I know, but there's no malicious intent. I'm not like that, you know?"

"I know, comrade, but since we have more freedom now to do much as we please, I suppose we have to be careful that we don't go over the top and take innocent pleasure to unhealthy excess."

"What a mind! And you're only fourteen. You could have become Prime Minister if you'd lived."

"I doubt it – I'd have settled for a Maths teacher or a scientist, pushing back the frontiers of knowledge," replied Eddie. "That would have been even better."

Almost unconsciously, the two boys had begun to make their way down Station Road and into town. Neither was interested in the time of year or, indeed, if it was still 1971. Their weighty discussion had made mundane things seem trivial. Fortunately, by the time they had reached the shopping area proper, Len had started to relax – it had clearly taken him some time to absorb all Eddie's friendly advice and to rid his mind of feelings of guilt and embarrassment. He cheered up quickly when he saw a poster in the East Shires Travel Agency.

"That would be fun, Captain, and we can't upset or harm anybody."

"What are you looking at?" asked Eddie as he peered over his shoulder.

"Parachute jumps at Beacon Hill Airbase; Saturday and Sunday afternoons at two – beginners welcome," said Len.

Eddie guessed where his friend's mind was going.

"You mean …?"

"Why not? We don't need a parachute."

"Need one? We wouldn't have one, you idiot!"

"Well, you should be O.K. – you've already done something similar a few years ago. Remember Paris and the Eiffel Tower?"

Eddie smiled as he did indeed recall a day in May 1963 when the two twelve-year-olds had taken their fantastic trip across Europe via France's capital. Eddie's special powers that day had allowed him to jump off the top of one of the world's tallest man-made structures and free-fall to the ground unharmed. Len's present suggestion would pale that into insignificance.

"Where is Beacon Hill, then?" asked Eddie at last. "I'll only go on two conditions, Len."

"Which are?"

"One: you behave and don't try anything funny and two: we try to get there by normal means; no spiriting us there again."

"Agreed, and the instructions for getting there are on the poster, if you look."

"But there is another problem, Len, my son."

"What?"

"Is today a Saturday or a Sunday? It didn't seem very likely with all the people getting off trains. They looked like they were off to work."

Len looked deflated, until another thought occurred to him.

"We don't actually need an aeroplane that's carrying parachutists. We could just hop aboard any aircraft that happens to be taking off."

"What kind of airbase is Beacon Hill, then?" queried Eddie.

"I think it's run jointly by the RAF and the US Air Force; the Yanks have jets and bombers that fly in and out. Fancy flying at Mach One, Biggles?"

"Now that sounds like fun," said Eddie, warming to the idea. Surely Len wouldn't try to interfere with the controls or anything else concerned with flying an aircraft. Then a worrying thought occurred to him. He couldn't think how he had missed the problem.

"You realise we have no mass or weight, Len, and remember the problem you had when that bloke removed his suitcase on the train."

"So what? We won't be sitting on suitcases," said Len.

"You're not thinking straight, Len. If we're standing or even sitting in the plane and then we somehow get out of the aircraft, we might just remain suspended in space like you were before. To all intents and purposes, the plane would be acting like the pile of suitcases as our contact is removed. And besides, you haven't explained to me how we would get out of the plane yet."

While Len frowned again, and despite his own misgivings, Eddie began to think that it would be fun to investigate the problem, in any case. Probably the worst that could happen was that they would disappear temporarily back to oblivion as Len had done on the train. They weren't doing anything bad after all; just trying an experiment. Then, Len had an answer to Eddie's question.

"We try thinking our way through the fuselage."

"And if that doesn't work?"

"And if that doesn't work, we forget the whole idea and stay in the plane until it lands."

"You promise you won't try anything else," said Eddie, sternly.

"Like what?"

"Like trying to make a door open. You could depressurise the cabin and kill people."

"I promise, Captain Biggles. I'm not that stupid."

"So how do we get there?"

Len pointed at the poster.

"Train from Hamsden to Seaton Market and a number 33 bus to Beacon village. The airbase is half a mile north of the village on the B1079."

"And what do we do when we find the airbase is surrounded by the inevitable ten foot high wire mesh fence and patrolled by American soldiers?" asked Eddie.

"So what's the problem? One of your conditions was that we should use ordinary methods of transport to get there. You didn't stipulate anything about what would happen when we got there, Captain. Why can't we just walk under or through the barrier or, failing that, walk through the fence?"

Eddie's earlier suggestion that it wasn't the weekend was quickly confirmed when they arrived back at Hamsden station. Wednesday, November the 15th 1972 promised to be a beautiful autumn day; crisp, sunny and with hardly a breeze to speak of. The rail and bus journey to the village of Beacon was smooth and uneventful with the two ghosts the only 'passengers' to alight at the terminus outside St Mary's Church. Within ten minutes they were standing outside the largely American airbase, having initially dared only to reach a position about one hundred yards from the main and closely-guarded entrance.

"It looks more like twelve feet than ten," said Eddie.

"So?" said Len, with no apparent concern. "Through here or up to the barrier and wander round it?"

Eddie looked hesitant and Len, failing to understand the reason, said,

"Are you still worried that we'll be seen, or something? We're invisible, for God's sake!"

"No, I'm just trying to keep our escapade as honest as I can – just to see how little or how much we need to use our special powers. It's like a real test, then, so that if we ever did have a problem we might be able to resolve it quickly and easily."

Hardly waiting for Eddie to finish stating his concerns, Len had already started walking boldly towards the barrier and guard boxes, one positioned on each side of the entrance. Eddie paused for a moment and then followed his friend. A big American car was just about to exit the base and, trying not to look at the guards, the boys strolled past while the barrier was still raised.

"Smooth as a nut," said Len. "There was never going to be a problem."

"*Hey, you guys, stop!*"

Eddie froze on the spot. Len looked back over his right shoulder.

"*Hey, bud, you forgot your ID.*"

"It's alright, Captain – he was talking to the driver."

Eddie didn't seem to be amused.

"Let's get out to the airfield quickly."

When the boys had covered the half mile or so needed to reach the runways, there didn't seem to be any flight activity going on. There appeared to be three landing strips, roughly forming a triangle with overlapping sides. One seemed to be under repair judging by the two or three JCBs and accompanying civilian workmen. The other two stood empty except for a huge military transport plane at one end.

"That looks a possibility," observed Len. "Plenty of room inside, if we needed any!"

"Can you make out what it is?" asked Eddie.

"Definitely one of theirs, judging by the markings. Let's get closer and I'll see if I can identify it – it's absolutely enormous."

Eddie knew that if anyone could tell what the plane was, it would be his friend, who had taken a keen interest in aircraft in his real life, provided that was, it hadn't been introduced after 1966.

"A Lockheed C-5 Galaxy, Captain!" exclaimed Len when they had got to within fifty yards of the enormous plane. Eddie's mouth dropped and remained open while he tried to gauge its actual dimensions.

"It's got to be at least the height of two houses and a hundred yards from wing tip to wing tip and about the same in length."

"You're right about the first bit – it's just over sixty feet high, but the wingspan and length from nose to tail are between seventy and eighty yards, if I remember correctly," replied Len, proudly. "And, it only needs just over a mile of runway to take off and land, which is not bad given it's about the largest plane in the world."

Suddenly, two of the four General Electric turbo engines roared and thundered into life. If Eddie and Len had been made of living flesh, they would have needed urgent surgery to their ears, but, instead, they watched in wonder, transfixed by the giant aircraft as it shuddered into life. The second two engines fired and Len brought them back to the reality of the moment.

"Quick, before they lift the cargo ramp."

The two ghosts bounded towards the gaping mouth at the front of the plane, jumping the last few feet to land safely on the ramp whose end was already three or feet off the ground. Once they had walked to the back of the aircraft, the two boys could easily see, by the empty cargo hold, that this was going to be no more than a training flight if, indeed, they weren't just testing the engines. Seconds after they had found sitting positions against some empty pallets, the huge nose configuration descended from its elevated position and the aircraft was sealed for flight.

"Shouldn't we be strapped in by some harnesses," queried Eddie.

"Don't be daft, mate, you should know we won't move – we didn't when we went to the moon."

And move they didn't, as minutes later the aerial monster lumbered down the runway and, defying gravity with extraordinarily consummate ease, lifted off the ground. Way up towards the front of the aircraft they could just hear the voice of the pilot communicating with the airbase, confirming their flight path and status.

"You do realise, Eddie, that if we do float down to earth, we'll have to get ourselves back to Hamsden by public transport if we're to stick to your rules," said Len.

This time, it was Eddie's turn to mock his friend's remark.

"Why? Is that where you live now? We don't have homes now, you numbskull. We can go anywhere we like until our batteries run dry and one or both of us go back to sleep. We may even just have to hang around for a while, and I mean that literally!"

After about twenty minutes of what seemed to be a fairly steep climb, the giant plane seemed to level out and Eddie listened carefully for an indication of their final cruising height.

"*It's a beautiful day up here, Beacon Two – our air speed is 417 knots and our altitude is 27,350 feet. Visibility is good. Please advise of any adverse weather on our height and heading.*"

"Roughly five miles up, Len, or nearly at the height of Everest."

Len gave his normal simple response.

"Wow!"

"It's highest I've been since we flew back from Poland in May 1963, Len."

"Me too, then, I suppose," replied Len. "Well, are we going to see what it's like outside?"

"Ye-es, if you're ready."

"I'm ready, Captain; just give the order."

"Roger, Navigator. Proceed to abandon the aircraft."

"Which way, Skip?"

Eddie pointed to the fuselage to their right.

"Let's try there."

The two ghosts stood up and moved slowly to the aircraft's side where they stopped when their faces were a few inches from the internal metal carcase. Eddie then said,

"We both walk forward together – on three, O.K?"

"Roger, Captain. Message received and understood."

Eddie started counting.

"One – two – three, go!"

Both ghosts closed their eyes and took a step forward. Len screamed with delight almost before the two boys found themselves suddenly in bright sunshine.

"I'm flying! I'm in the air!"

Eddie watched as the Galaxy shot forward at over four hundred miles an hour. They were suspended in space at nearly 30,000 feet and their transport had left them; it was already heading for the horizon. His friend's 'body' was about five yards in front if him and slightly to his left. He seemed frozen in his last act of movement, with legs astride and arms front and back. Though he couldn't seem to move his head, and felt also that his own body must be fixed in a similar position to his friend's, he was able to respond verbally.

"Well, not exactly flying, Mr Navigator – just floating, and I think therefore my guess was right. We can't fall."

Expecting both their bodies to 'freeze' completely and even the power of speech to disappear, Eddie was mildly surprised when Len seemed able to swivel his body in order to face him.

"How did you do that?"

Len moved gracefully over to Eddie, almost as though he was just swimming in the sea off Fenton beach.

"Easy – I cheated and concentrated my mind on turning round and coming over to you."

"So my experiment has worked," said Eddie. "We can't seem to defy the normal laws of science. Zero mass; zero weight; zero acceleration."

"Whatever you say, Einstein. More importantly right now, are we going to try to think our way to the ground?"

Ten minutes before the Lockheed C-5 Galaxy had left the ground at Beacon Hill airbase, British Midland Airways flight number BM201 had taken off from Manchester airport at 11.40 heading south for London Heathrow. The newly operational Boeing 707 was only half-full; the rest of its passengers would be boarding in the capital for the fully-booked three-hour flight to Majorca for some late autumn warmth. At 12.30 precisely, its complement of seventy-eight passengers and crew were increased by the addition of two invisible non-paying guests.

Eddie and Len had tried in vain for several minutes to get their bodies to move vertically downwards, but their only permissible motion proved to be in a horizontal direction. Whatever power was in overall control that morning, they were able to rendezvous with the 707 over the Cambridgeshire fens. As Eddie would admit later, the chances of them having been at precisely the same necessary height were millions to one. Fortunately their lateral speed proved to be sufficient to complete the rendezvous within a few seconds of Len spotting the Boeing from several hundred yards away. Their final entrance into the plane was as easy as had been their exit from the Galaxy a short time earlier.

At ten to one, flight BM201 commenced its approach into London Heathrow. Eddie and Len had found two rear seats with only one flight attendant for company.

"So, we're landing at Heathrow, Captain? That manoeuvre was out of this world, almost like we were meant to do it."

"Yes, Navigator; you did a good job, but I think you're right – we had a little help I suspect. God certainly does moves in a mysterious way and it's still only lunchtime. Pity we can't sample the airport food, eh?"

"It's sleep I need," said Len. "I'm bushed."

As his friend made his remark, Eddie watched as Len's body faded into nothingness. He had been granted his request. It had been a good day, thought Eddie. Len had behaved himself and an interesting experiment had been accomplished. What would happen to him when the plane landed at Heathrow and where would he go next? He closed his eyes to think of the possibilities.

13
Confirmation of Evil

By the time Christmas was approaching in 1973, little Ed had grown into a chubby, freckly and ginger-headed four-year-old, who loved nothing more than to accompany his grandma when she went shopping in Fenton-on-Sea. He hadn't inherited all of his late uncle's characteristics; he clearly wasn't going to be skinny or indeed, shy. Though Eddie's sister and her son had moved out from her parents' home earlier that year – when Jenny's divorce from Gary had finally come through – Ann Compton often helped her daughter by looking after her grandson while Jenny was at work. Christmas Eve was always a busy time at 'Curls and Twirls' and, with no pre-school playgroup to go to, Jenny's mum had little Ed until three that afternoon. During term-time, Jenny still only worked mornings so she could collect little Ed at lunchtime. During the holidays she had to manage as best she could, using a combination of her mum and a couple of local neighbours on her modern housing estate, conveniently situated just north of the avenues where Fir Tree Close was located. She was only renting – a compact two-bedroom semi, but its proximity to her parents' house meant that she could walk Ed down there before she caught the train to Hamsden. Gary had moved away from the area and saw his son only very occasionally. After the less than amicable divorce, he seemed to lose interest in the upbringing and welfare of little Ed, confirming the original disinterest when he had been born.

Ann Compton had some last minute shopping to do in Fenton that Christmas Eve morning and little Ed was clearly excited at the prospect, after Jenny had left him with his grandma at just after eight o'clock. Fred Compton had left for work early at seven-thirty because of the likely rush of last minute passengers. By nine, Jenny's mum was doing some dusting with little Ed as her number one helper. The cleaning team had reached the lounge where little Ed was always given the responsibility of cleaning his uncle's photograph and frame.

"Nanny?"

"Yes, Ed."

"Nanny, can we go to Woolworth's?"

"Probably, love."

"Will Father C'ismas be there?"

"I don't know; I expect so, but only if you've been good. He doesn't see naughty little boys."

Ed went silent and after a pause, he said,

"Mummy says it was only an accident."

"What was, dear?"

"I b'oke a plate, Grandma. I didn't mean to."

"Of course you didn't but don't break Uncle Eddie, alright?"

"No, Grandma."

Little Ed paused at he gazed at his uncle's image.

"Was Uncle Eddie always good, Grandma?"

"Yes, dear, most of the time."

"What was the baddest thing he ever, ever did?"

Ann Compton wanted to say something like: '*Running away from home and leaving me and Grandad*', but she said instead,

"Oh, I don't know; coming in late with his clothes dirty or not concentrating in English at school."

"That's not very bad, Grandma. I always get my things dirty."

"It was for him, my little love."

Little Ed gave Uncle Eddie back for his grandma to return him to his place on the wall and said,

"I wish Uncle Eddie would come back, Grandma."

"So do I, little Ed. So do I."

By ten-thirty, little Ed and his grandmother had started to make their way out of Fir Tree Close and into South Road. It was cold and frosty with ice still on the ground. Despite having recently had his fourth birthday, little Ed still helped take his pushchair on any trip into town. He rarely got in it anymore and it seemed now to be needed only as some form of comforter or pal for him. This morning it gave him added stability on his little chubby legs with some of the roads and paths still icy. Ann Compton found it invaluable for carrying her shopping and handbag. This particular morning, she had been looking forward, for some time, to a very rare visit to Russell Jones' in the High Street, conveniently located directly opposite her grandson's favourite destination. Russell Jones' was, for Fenton-on-Sea, a fairly chic and modern fashion shop and Ann had had her eye on a particular blouse and skirt for Christmas Day. Her grandson, of course, had other ideas when they reached the door to the dress shop.

"Woolworth's, Grandma. There's Woolworth's. San'a! San'a! San'a!" he gabbled, tugging at Ann Compton's sleeve."

"In a minute, Ed, love. Just wait until Grandma has done her shopping. Then we'll go and see Father Christmas."

It would be over half an hour before grandma and grandson would emerge from Russell Jones' and, when they did so, little Ed was understandably anxious and excited.

Little Ed's namesake had woken from his slumbers at almost precisely the same time as the two shoppers had entered Russell Jones'. Eddie was quite excited to find that it was Christmas time and the last day before the big day as well. That excitement was enhanced by the nostalgic surroundings he had found himself in – the very shop that was little Ed's favourite as it had also been his when he had been his nephew's age. Eddie found the next half an hour quite absorbing as he wandered round the shop, looking at all the modern toys and games for sale. Surely it would not be long until his friend joined him, given all the memories of those times when, on a Saturday, he and Len would spend their pocket money, or just wander round the shop looking at all the things they wanted but couldn't afford. When it became clear to Eddie that Len wasn't in Woolworth's, he headed for the door to the High Street where, to his great surprise and joy, he immediately spotted his mum and little nephew emerging from Russell Jones'. He desperately wanted to shout out a greeting, but instead, he had to watch in horror as little Ed wrested his hand from his grandma's grasp and ran into the road. It seemed to Eddie that his little nephew appeared very excited and was shouting something as he left the pavement. Though it was difficult to read the little boy's lips at that distance, Eddie had the distinct sense that he was saying something like,

'*Uncle Eddie! Santa, Uncle Eddie! Santa*!'

Had it not been so icy, little Ed would probably have got across the road safely that morning. As it was, with his grandma screaming for all she was worth, he slipped and fell to the ground right in the middle of the road. The nightmare immediately got worse as Eddie watched, in slow motion, as his nephew disappeared under the front wheels of a single-decker bus, whose driver had been trying desperately to pull up from fifty yards further up the High Street. The number 201 slewed sideways, its rear end colliding with Ann Compton and her pushchair, throwing them both into Russell Jones' window. Glass could be heard shattering as the bus then followed suit. The whole event had unfolded in less a matter of seconds. Thankfully, with the bus obscuring his view, Eddie could no longer see either his mother or his nephew, but he knew he faced the harsh reality that neither could have survived such a horrendous accident. People were rushing from all directions.

"Get an ambulance!"

"Get out of the way – I'm a doctor!"

"Good trick, Ed, eh? Best one so far. I told you I'd be back and you couldn't get rid of me."

Eddie glanced to his right. Evil had returned. Len was grinning from ear to ear with his arms folded across his chest in a triumphant pose that said, '*I did that – I can do anything*'.

"You murdering devil!" screamed Eddie. "Murderer!"

"How do you know they're dead, Ed? It might be far worse; they might be maimed for life and wish that they had died. Shall I go and see and finish the job off? Dead Ed, eh? That even rhymes. Dead Ed, dead Ed dead …."

Pure evil was chanting and it had to be defeated. Eddie closed his eyes, fell to his knees and prayed.

"Oh God, please save Mum and little Ed. Please make them alright and send the devil away. Please, oh God, I beg you. Save my mum and nephew."

"Hi ya, Eddie. What are you doing, Captain?"

"Go away, you murderer. Get thee me behind me, Satan!"

"What are you talking about, mate? It's me, Len."

Still Eddie remained on his knees and repeated his supplication. The screams and noises had stopped, but there was no sound of an ambulance coming. '*Where, oh where is the ambulance?*' thought Eddie. He dared to raise his head and open his eyes. His mother and nephew were still standing on the opposite side of the High Street, waiting for a single-decker 201 bus to pass, as its driver steered it gingerly over the icy surface. If Eddie could have cried at that moment, he would have shed an ocean of tears as the realisation of what had happened sunk home. Evil had returned to display its power, but Good had triumphed in the end. Len's good ghost was still standing at his side and said,

"What was that all about, mate? Looked to me like you were praying. Anyway, what did 'Buzz' Aldrin say when he first stepped on the moon in 1969, Captain?"

"Monterey Jack or New Jersey Blue, then?" mumbled Eddie. "Oh God, Len, you won't believe what's just happened."

"Hey, that's your mum, Eddie, isn't it? Just walked past us into Woolies. Is that your nephew, then?"

"Yes, Len, that's little Ed."

"Wow! He looks like you, old son."

14
More Confetti

It wasn't to be very much longer that cold Christmas Eve before Eddie began to feel tired after such an emotional and terrifying experience. He and Len had followed Eddie's mum and nephew back into Woolworth's, though Eddie hardly had the concentration to pay much attention to his friend's curiosity about his mum and nephew. Len was particularly taken with the family likeness that little Ed had acquired.

"He's got your hair, but your sister's face. He's going to be a bit fatter than you as well."

"Anyone would be fatter than me," replied Eddie. "I was always skinny until I …."

"Your mum looks happy, too, mate," continued Len.

"Yeah, I think she must enjoy being a grandmother. Don't you want to see your mum again?"

"Not until just now when I saw yours, Eddie. I often wonder if she ever married again."

Eddie didn't reply immediately to his friend's rhetorical question – he recalled the wake after the funerals of Cyril Wilby and his son. Martha Wilby had been engaged in deep conversation with a strange man then, who had seemed to Eddie at the time to have been more than just a distant friend. Also, though he had just managed to hold a conversation with Len, his mind was still spinning from what he had just witnessed and the horrible trick that his friend's evil ghost had just performed – that friend who was cheerfully taking to him at his side.

"I think next time I come back I should definitely like to go and see her again. Find out how she is, you know," continued Len when his friend remained silent.

"What? Oh yes – good idea, mate. I'll come with you if I'm allowed."

"Allowed?" asked Len.

"Yeah, if God allows us to meet up again soon."

"You and your God, Len. Are you certain he's doing all this for us?"

And then, at last, Eddie at last managed to blurt out all about the extraordinary event that had taken place outside in the High Street a short time earlier.

"Oh, I'm sorry, mate. I didn't realise. You don't think I had anything to do with it, do you?"

"No, but …."

Len's head drooped, and when Eddie didn't continue, he said,

"You do, don't you? You do think I knew it was happening."

"I don't know, Len. I'm tired."

Len began to get angry.

"Eddie, I'm your best friend, mate, for goodness sake. What on earth are you saying? That I'm evil? That I know what my bad side is doing? We've all got a bad side – or don't you even believe that?"

"I told you, I don't know what I think. I know we can all be bad, but your evil ghost is still part of you and it seems to want to dominate you. You mustn't let it do that, Len."

Len looked genuinely upset now and said,

"And how do I do that? I'm not trying to be bad, if that's what you believe. Something outside of me must be trying to take me over and I can't feel it happening – honest, Eddie. You have to believe me and help me. I don't know what to do."

"Just trust and believe that God can beat him for you – that he can erase him from your soul or as much of him as to render him harmless. Put you faith in God. He won't let you down, Len."

Eddie wasn't sure whether Len had absorbed his friendly advice as he felt his body begin to shut down and return to temporary oblivion. Somewhere in the distance he thought and hoped that he heard Len say,

"I will put my trust in God, Eddie. From now on I will be good."

However good Len's intentions were in eventually deciding to go and see his mum, he would later discover that there was always going to be a potentially difficult problem in trying to achieve his somewhat belated wish. Martha Wilby had quickly decided after the tragic double loss of her husband, Cyril, and her son, that she would try to get on with the rest of her life with a positive attitude. The role of a grieving widow and mother was not going to be her métier for the rest of her days. Indeed, within the first few months of her double tragedy, she had become not only a woman of substance, but also one who was determined to make the best of her not unattractive looks. Cyril Wilby had left her well-provided for – enough for her to lead an independent life of leisure combined with church voluntary work. By Christmas of her annus horribilus, she had attracted one or two admirers in the small north Kent seaside town of Petersgate, where as a family the Wilbys had moved only a matter of weeks before they were to be reduced from three to one. Her one special admirer, however, did not live in Petersgate, nor was he a recent acquisition. Michael Conners had known Martha Wilby for more than fifteen years, ever since she and her husband had been colleagues at a secondary school in the London's East End. Cyril had been a woodwork teacher and Martha a cook in the school kitchen. Michael Conners had been the sole attendee from the Wilby's previous school at the double funeral in late August 1965 and afterwards, the two former colleagues began a telephone/letter-writing relationship. By the end of 1967 it had blossomed into something more tangible, and for the next five years, whilst still spending the majority of their lives as individuals in different locations, they spent an ever-increasing minority in each other's company, both in Petersgate and in Whitechapel. Several holidays at home and abroad were taken in tandem and by the summer of 1973, on one romantic trip to Paris, Michael Conners proposed to Martha Wilby. She hesitated only for a couple of seconds before responding in the affirmative. They were both fifty-three years old.

Decisions had to be taken over where they were to live after their marriage, planned for April the 6th the following year. Michael still had up to another seven years to go before his retirement from his post as Head of Humanities at Friar Lane Comprehensive. For her part, Martha didn't really want to sell her house in Petersgate which would be an excellent retirement area when her husband-to-be reached that time. In the end, the couple decided to live in Michael's bungalow in Whitechapel until his retirement, while 23 The Park would be rented out until the couple moved back when Michael retired. They chose to rent it to some students – a young married couple who would only use it in term time, leaving it available for their own use in the school holidays. If not perfect, it seemed to be the best compromise, given that Michael needed to be near his work for a few years. Martha and Michael moved in together in the London bungalow a few days before Christmas and 23 The Park was rented to two medical students from early January 1974. Martha had given in to Michael over the venue for the wedding and it was booked for one p.m. on Saturday, April the 6th at St Margaret's Parish Church just off Brick Lane. The reception was to be at the Garden Hotel in Sebastopol Square at two-thirty. It would be a small gathering – less then thirty guests, most of whom were Michael's friends and family. Martha's sister and her husband were her only relations to be invited. Apart from her old friends from Fenton-on-Sea, Fred and Ann Compton, Martha would only have a few other representatives, all from St Michael's Church in Petersgate, where she had worshipped before moving to Whitechapel.

Before he left for his welcome rest after his friend's bombardment of his conscience, Len had made up his mind that he really did want to visit his mother on the next occasion he was raised to 'life'. As consciousness left him that Christmas Eve, his mind offered up a silent prayer to extend his verbal testimony of a split second earlier. However, he would have to pass a difficult test if he was to accomplish his desire – a test that would, once and for all, establish the genuineness and sincerity of his aspiration to see his mother once more.

It was nine-thirty on a bright but chilly April morning when next he awoke to the land of the living. His surroundings were familiar to him, though that familiarity had not been long established before he had departed his natural life. Before his eyes were allowed to open, however, his ears were presented with unfamiliar voices – ones that his mind was certain it was not acquainted with.

"Are you going to work this morning, Phil?"

"No, I thought I'd leave that project on brain tumours until tomorrow. Prof Micklesen doesn't want to discuss it for at least another week. How about you, love?"

"No, I've just one experiment to write up and I can do that when you do your work. Let's go out for the day. I fancy doing some shopping in Canterbury with a spot of lunch at the Bishop's Finger."

Len could see by now and he found he was sitting in a pleasant and familiar room. His eyes immediately focused on a couple of framed photographs standing on a table to his side. One was familiar; one was not. The one he recognised was of himself and his dad, taken outside their old house in Fenton-on-Sea on the very morning of their move to Kent. The second photo was also of a man of similar age to Cyril Wilby, but unknown to Len. Then Len knew where he was. It had to be the lounge of his new house in Petersgate; the house that he and his dad had left that fateful day in August 1965 to go fishing off Deal pier; the house from which his mother had returned after burying her husband and son on the same day and the house that now seemed occupied by other people.

"Right, love, I'll just have a quick shower and we'll be off in ten minutes," said Phil.

"O.K. – that's great."

Len had quickly decided that the young couple must be students and very much in love as they made their way out of the lounge to get ready for their trip to Canterbury. Within a quarter of an hour, he had the house to himself. Despite his invisibility, he had remained in his position in the lounge until he had heard a car pull out of the drive of 23 The Park, Petersgate.

Though there were many familiar things belonging to his mother in the house, its general untidiness told Len that his mother was no longer living there. For several minutes Len couldn't work out what the apparent contradiction could mean. If she had moved, why had she left many of her possessions let alone most of her furniture? Although it had been nearly eight years since he had been inside the house, and the decor had changed, it still had his mother's stamp on it, but where was she? What had caused her to leave everything behind when she had left? But had she left? It would have made sense to Len at that moment if his mother had taken in the students for the added income the rent would provide her. He leapt up and ran upstairs to his mother's bedroom, passing piles of books and folders on the stairs – his mother just couldn't be renting to these students; not if she was still living here.

Not only was his mother's bedroom clearly being used by the two students, but also the other two rooms were not even fitted out as bedrooms. One, his former room, seemed to be an office and the second was piled high with boxes and general junk. 'No', thought Len as he returned downstairs, 'Mum is not living here anymore'. It was ten past ten and Len was beginning to get a strong feeling that he was in the wrong place and needed to be elsewhere that morning. He started to look for any clues as to where his mum might have gone. He began in the kitchen where he remembered his mother always kept a message board, on which she used to leave him notes or jot down important reminders. Though the cork board was still there, it contained nothing of relevance for Len. The calendar for 1974, hanging next to the board, also contained no clues to his mother's whereabouts except to answer one question that had concerned him. A note had been made in the space for April the 1st, which read, '*Rent due – send cheque to Mrs Wilby.*' So, his mother still owned the house and was indeed renting it to the two medical students. Nothing else in the kitchen gave any indication of a forwarding address for the rent or mail and Len returned to the lounge for any clues as to where his mother might be living. He found nothing of use, unable as he was to move or pick things up. With nothing else in mind, other than curiosity, he looked in more detail at the photograph of the strange man on the small table. To his surprise, and perhaps by a slice of preordained luck, he found a slim pocket-sized diary for 1974 lying open behind it. By walking round to the side of the table, he could just read what was written on the two open pages. At first, with '*University of Canterbury*' stamped at the top of each page, it didn't at first suggest it would be much use, but at least the owner seemed to be an avid recorder of anything and everything. The entry for April the 6th – the probable date that day, given the calendar in the kitchen – was plain enough even for him to read. What he read there gave him another reason to the question as to why his mother was not there. The entry read:

'Mrs Wilby's wedding, St Margaret's, Whitechapel'.

Underneath, and in a different hand, someone else had written:

'And we're not invited'.

Len took a step backwards. His mother was getting remarried and, no doubt, to the man in the photograph, and the wedding was that very day. He knew at once that, not only must he try to get there, he was also expected to get there. Everything pointed to it – his arrival at his mother's house on the precise date and the pure chance that the diary had given him the details. It all made sense. It was now half past ten and he had to get a move on. When *was* the ceremony and could he get there on time? He knew more or less where the church was, from the time he had lived with his mum and dad in the East End, but how was he to get to Whitechapel? He made for the locked front door and, to his relief, walked right through it and out into The Park. No time for niceties today, he thought, even though Eddie might not approve. His hazy memory of his three-week residency led him into the town and the railway station. By chance (?), the London train was due to leave at ten to the hour and Len slipped aboard behind two young ladies. The train was less than half-full and Len was able to find a seat with ease.

Nothing happened to concern Len until the train reached Chatham at twelve-fifteen, when it was swelled to capacity by the many shoppers bound for the city. He made himself scarce by occupying, as usual, the space next to an exit door. By the time the train pulled into Victoria, something was telling him that he was late and that the wedding was about to begin without him. Running down the platform at the station with the clock reading 12.57, he tried to consider his options. He knew roughly how to get to Whitechapel, but wasn't there an easier way? What would Eddie have done? He passed through the ticket barrier and suddenly remembered what his friend's last words to him had been:

'*Put your faith in God. He won't let you down*'.

Len stopped running and bowed his head. With no one other than the intended recipient to hear, he said out loud,

"Please God; get me to my mum's wedding. Please, oh please, get me there. I truly believe that you can do it."

The last sound that he heard as his special transport whisked him away from Victoria was a clock sounding the hour.

St Margaret's Church was barely a quarter full for the one o'clock ceremony; twenty-nine wedding guests, eleven regular parishioners, four church helpers, two churchwardens, a photographer, the organist, the bride, the groom , the best man, a lone photographer and the Reverend Bob Anderson made up the entire congregation – in all fifty-three living souls. In addition, one dead soul stood smiling invisibly directly behind the Reverend Anderson.

Like Eddie had been at his sister's wedding four and a half years previously, Len was both proud of and amazed by his mother's radiance and poise. If it had been possible, there would have been a tear in his eye when the wedding vows were exchanged. It warmed Len's ghostly heart to see his mother so obviously happy with her new man and he even hoped that his dad, Cyril, was looking down and giving his seal of approval to her new marriage. Len knew her dead husband would have wanted her to be happy.

"*And I am, son.*"

Almost without thinking, Len replied to the voice out loud,

"What? Are you here, Dad?"

"I'm right behind you, son."

Len turned round to see his dad. He looked exactly as had that fatal summer Sunday in 1965. Like his son, he hadn't aged a bit and he looked happy with his wife's decision to remarry.

"I'm glad your mum did this today. I knew Michael at Friar Lane; he was a History teacher when I was there. He was a nice man and I always suspected he had a soft spot for your mother."

By this time, Mendelssohn's Wedding March was accompanying the new Mr and Mrs Conners down the aisle and Len and his dad slipped cheekily in behind them.

"Where's the reception, Dad?" asked Len as they fitted in step with the happy couple.

"Don't know, Len. I only arrived a few minutes ago when you thought of me, I guess."

"Didn't you know you were coming, then, Dad?"

"No – this is my first visit back to the living world."

"Really?" queried Len. "Where have you been?"

"Nowhere, Len. In my grave, I suppose, if your mum had me buried."

"She did," said Len, as father and son emerged from the church into drizzle that had just started to fall. Neither of them seemed to be certain of what to do next, until Len said,

"We'll just have to jump into one of the cars, Dad."

"There won't be room, son. All the places will be taken."

And then Len burst out laughing. His dad was new to this game, he thought.

"Dad – we're ghosts! We don't occupy space. If we sit on someone's lap, they wouldn't feel a thing. Which lady do you fancy?"

"Len! Don't be rude."

Len smiled. His dad still thought he was fourteen, even though his mind had aged. He played along.

"Sorry, Dad. Here, be quick, there's room in that one."

Len led his dad to a red Datsun and, while the driver put a wedding present on the back seat, the two ghosts followed it in before the door closed behind them. The car moved off with a sudden jerk, causing the woman passenger to say,

"Careful, Fred, you'll break the vase in the back."

"Sorry, love, I'm still haven't got used to the clutch."

"Dad! It's Eddie's mum and dad."

Fred glanced in his rear-view mirror and nearly floored the accelerator.

"Oh my God, it's …."

"It can't be, Len."

"What are you doing, Fred?"

"It is, Dad – it's Uncle Fred and Aunty Ann and Uncle Fred's seen you."

The car came to an abrupt halt as Fred pulled the car to the kerb. He turned round and said,

"Oh, God, it's happening again, love."

"What is, love?"

"I thought I saw Cyril Wilby and Len in the back seat."

"Told you, Dad."

Ann Compton looked round.

"There's no one there, Fred. It's your mind playing tricks again for the umpteenth time. You really should go and see someone."

"There's no one there now, but I'm sure there was."

"I really am a ghost now, son."

"Yes, Dad – you are."

The car pulled away from the kerb.

"It was just your mind, love. It's been a while since we've seen Martha and memories of Cyril and Len would have come back to you, that's all. Made you see things that aren't there."

"You're right, love."

"No she's not Uncle Fred. Oh no, she's not."

Cyril Wilby and his son could easily have walked to the Garden Hotel – Sebastopol Square was less than half a mile from the church and Len's dad had clearly been there before.

"We used to have our staff end-of-term parties here, Len. Years ago now, but it hasn't changed much," he said as they stood outside the hotel.

The two ghosts had just jumped out of the car, using the opportunity provided by Ann Compton when she had opened a rear door to retrieve her wedding present. This normal type of exit from the car had been a close run thing, and Len knew that he could have shown his dad his extra powers and just emerged through the locked door. There would be time for a demonstration when his dad was more accustomed to his new role.

Fred and Ann Compton found that, apart from Martha, they really knew no one else at the reception. They had met Martha's sister at the funeral, but that had been nearly nine years ago. While the wedding lunch was comfortable enough for them, being a sit-down affair, the after-lunch party was less so. Never a couple to socialise easily with strangers, they ended up fairly isolated at a small table for four in one corner of the intimate hotel room – isolated, that was, apart from their two observers.

Fred had already had a pint and a glass and a half of champagne by the end of the meal and once he changed to fruit juice, he seemed to become fidgety and somewhat agitated. He had wanted to have a couple of stiff whiskies, but Ann Compton had put her foot down, given that he would be driving them back to Fenton-on-Sea at about six. Downing his third orange juice, he looked at his watch.

"Ten to five, love. We ought to be making a move – try to get home before dark."

"We can't go yet, Fred," said Ann. "Not before Martha and Michael leave for Paris at six. It wouldn't be right."

"No, you can't Uncle Fred – you've got to see Aunty Martha off and throw some confetti."

Cyril Wilby and his son had spent most of the time since they'd been at the reception, watching and listening to the various conversations. Len's dad had found it particularly absorbing to move from group to group, comparing and contrasting opinions on all things from their fellow guests to the suitability of the happy couple. Len had hardly said a word in that time as he watched his dad become more accustomed to his role and, whenever he tried to tell his dad about all the adventures that he and Eddie had been on since the accident, he seemed either totally disinterested or downright sceptical, uttering dismissive comments to suggest that his son had simply dreamt the events. Soon, Len had given up, having decided that his dad probably wasn't going to be receptive to such adventures until he had experienced similar ones himself.

"Oh I need a real drink," said Fred.

"No, Fred," said his wife. "You've got to drive me home and you've already had enough. What is the matter? You don't usually drink at events like this. Still seeing things? Because if so, the drink will only make it worse."

"Not since the car. I just feel odd – need calming down, I suppose."

"Odd? What do you mean – odd?"

"Just not right, as though someone is watching me, love."

"Watching you?"

"Don't keep repeating what I say," replied Fred. "You sound like a parrot."

"Oh, sorry. I'm only trying to help, Fred," said Ann, irritably.

"Well, don't."

"Let's go, Dad, and leave them alone. I think Uncle Fred can sense us."

"O.K., son, let's go and listen to your mother."

For the next ten minutes, Fred and Ann Compton sat in silence, after which time, Fred seemed to have recovered his composure and got up to get himself another orange juice. When he had sat down again, he said,

"Sorry, love. I didn't mean to snap. I'm O.K. now – I'll be much better when we get back to Fenton."

Ann Compton patted her husband's hand and said,

"Just relax now, love, it's nearly half past five."

By the time Len and his dad went to look for Martha, she and her new husband seemed to have disappeared. Only by listening to Martha's sister did they realise that the happy couple had gone somewhere else in the hotel to change into their going-away clothes. Though his mother hadn't got married in a traditional white wedding dress, the outfit didn't look comfortable enough for travelling. They returned a few minutes before six to cheers and final goodbyes before they emerged from the hotel into the ever-persistent drizzle. Within a minute or so, their changes of clothes

186

were wet and peppered with confetti which stuck to them like sequins. The taxi whisked them away to a chorus of friendly farewells.

"Don't do anything I wouldn't do!"

"*You'd better look after her, Michael, or you'll have Len and I to answer to.*"

"Have a great time in gay Paris!"

"*I love you, Mum. Please don't forget me.*"

"*Or me, love. I'll always love you, Martha.*"

Cyril Wilby had already turned away by the time Martha waved back at him and mouthed, '*I love you, too, Cyril*'. Len returned his mother's wave on his father's behalf and nodded his acknowledgement.

15

Viking

Eddie sensed a certain finality when he next paid a visit to the real world. Much that had happened to him over the previous nine years of earth time had begun to make him believe that all the good and bad adventures had only been a precursor to something more important. Living a 'Heaven on Earth' was a wonderful experience and was probably only given to a privileged few, but there was only so much you could enjoy. With some of the frightening encounters he had had with evil, he was beginning to look forward to a more permanent sleep each time he returned to the peace of oblivion. He had even begun to think that that peaceful oblivion was a kind of heaven, too.

Eddie had soon realised on this, his latest visit, that it had indeed been over nine years since his tragic, but legitimate, departure from the real world. It was the 20th of August, 1975, as he wandered aimlessly past the railway station in Fenton-on-Sea on the opposite side of the High Street. Two minutes earlier, he had confirmed the date by looking at the newspapers on the rack outside Johnson's the newsagents. Another headline in one of the papers had also attracted his eye and, though it had only warranted a small portion of a front page, it had registered itself in Eddie's mind for later consideration. It seemed to be late afternoon and, pausing outside the station, he observed from the clock that the time was five-thirty.

While ambling up the High Street he had gained the strange but distinct feeling that this was going to be the last visit to his home town. Almost as if to remind him what Fenton-on-Sea had meant to him, he spotted a familiar figure coming out of the station forecourt. Fred Compton was leaving work as usual on this Wednesday. Eddie crossed over the road and started to follow his dad. Whether his feelings of finality were imagined or not, at that particular moment, he felt he needed to say goodbye to his family for one last time.

When Eddie reached number 38 Fir Tree Close, it was soon obvious that his mum and dad had visitors for tea. He had kept a fair distance behind his dad all the way back from the station but he couldn't fail to see, or hear, his young nephew running down the front path to greet his Grandad.

"Grandad! Grandad! We've come for tea and Mum says we can play with the train set."

Little Ed rushed into Fred Compton's arms just as Eddie reached the front gate. Several thoughts rushed into his head. The first thing that struck Eddie was that Ed's hair had changed from ginger to a deep brown; the second was how much he had grown. He clearly wasn't going to be skinny like his uncle, and his earlier chubbiness had been replaced by an unusually athletic build for a boy of five. The third thought brought memories flooding back to him; memories of his own train set and all the adventures it had provided. Then, the final thought hit him: '*Was it his own set that Ed had mentioned*?'

Grandad and Grandson walked hand in hand up the path and into the house while Eddie paused to prepare himself for seeing his family. After a few moments he wandered up the path and through the closed door. It was obvious from the crying that was coming from the lounge that Ed's request had been temporarily refused until after tea. Smiling to himself, Eddie made for the kitchen where he found his mum making sandwiches. Suddenly, as he stood watching her, he began to feel that he was intruding on a different life and a different time. The feeling got stronger the longer he gazed at his mother. Her whole demeanour seemed frozen in time – a very different time. As if to confirm his earlier feelings, the realisation suddenly hit him that he didn't actually want to stay long in the house – a place where he didn't now belong with the people that had meant so much to him in the past. It had been a mistake to come back – he had moved on. On a sudden impulse, he walked straight through the adjoining wall to the lounge where he found Ed, Jenny and her dad. Ed had dried his tears and was sitting next to his Grandad on the settee. His sister was reading a magazine. Half-expecting his nephew to acknowledge his presence as he had once done before, Eddie slid into the spare armchair. As he listened to the normal family conversation, Eddie's feeling that he was intruding began to sharpen. He didn't want to stay where there were so many memories, and he definitely didn't want to watch his nephew playing 'trains' with his Grandad, particularly if it was his own old *Flying Scotsman* set. He just didn't feel comfortable – he felt awkward and unable, of course, to join in the conversation. When his mother called from the kitchen he'd had enough.

"Ed, tea's ready!"

Before anyone had a chance to get up in response to Ann Compton's announcement, Eddie mouthed an '*I love you*' in three different directions and strode purposefully out of the room. He made the same gesture in front of his mum as she carried a plate of sandwiches through into the dining room. When he got to the front door, he turned back and though nobody could hear, he shouted at the top of his voice,

"*Goodbye Mum, Dad, Jenny and Ed! I'll love you forever.*"

He then turned and walked through the door behind him, praying it wouldn't bar his progress. He didn't stop until he reached the road outside the house where he was hit with the final realisation that he would never see any of his family again. That was, until ….

As he sauntered his way back towards the town, it seemed to Eddie that he had reached a crossroads in his new life. His former earthly existence, highlighted by the meeting with his family, seemed to matter less to him now – it had to be time to move to the next level of his new one. Other questions came to him. What if he wasn't going to remain a ghost forever? What if he went back to oblivion and stayed there for eternity? Like a prisoner on death row, he wanted to do as much as he could before his present 'heavenly' existence changed. God's universe was vast and even infinite and he was still confined to a tiny corner of it. There had to be more that his special powers would allow him to do. What more fun was there to be had in his ghostly role before his powers diminished or even expired completely?

"*Good evening, Captain.*"

Eddie had reached the High Street and hadn't noticed Len suddenly walking beside him. He was quick with his check.

"Before you say anything else, Len; what was the first thing 'Buzz' Aldrin said after he walked on the moon in 1969?"

"Monterey Jack or New Jersey Blue, then? Yes, it is me, Eddie."

"Good; I've things to tell you."

Eddie then shared all his most recent thoughts on their present ghostly existence and, after his friend had listened in silence all the way down to the foot of Steep Hill, he was mildly surprised by his response.

"Yeah, I've been thinking the same thing, too."

"You mean you're ready to leave this earth even it meant that you might never come back?"

"Yep – like you say we have powers that ought to be able to take us anywhere in the universe, or beyond."

"Beyond?"

"Why not? Who knows what's out there? I mean, we got to the moon, didn't we?"

"What about you mum? Don't you want to go and see her?"

"Done it. Saw her get married last April the last time I awoke."

"Really?"

And then it was Len's turn to share the details of his visit the year before, concluding with,

"So, I told her that I loved her. I know she'll be happy, so there's nothing really to keep me here now. Tottenham are never going to win the league."

Len paused and then asked,

"Do you have anything in mind for our last meal, as you called it?"

Then the headline came back to him: '*Mars launch tonight*'. Suddenly, St Andrew's Church clock started striking the hour. Eddie counted.

"Well?" said Len. "Do you?"

"Six, seven – seven o'clock. Sorry, Len. Yes, I might have."

"Well, are you going to tell me, or are you just going to check the time?"

"I needed to know, Len – if we're to catch the rocket that's taking the orbiter and lander to Mars. It takes off from Cape Canaveral at about twenty past ten this evening our time."

"You are joking, aren't you?"

"No, I'm not joking, Len."

By ten past seven, the two boys had wandered down to the water's edge to prepare for the transglobal attempt. Eddie had insisted that they stand on the beach at more or less the same spot where they had left Fenton-on-Sea twelve years previously for the first of their fantastic adventures. It had taken some time for their thought messages to get through to their 'mission control' – Len's name for the ultimate power that was guiding them. In the end, with Eddie beseeching his own 'ultimate power', and his friend eventually concurring, the two ghosts vanished from their former seaside home. Eddie's last action was to turn and look at the reassuring image of St Andrew's Church, standing firm and proud atop the cliffs behind him. It provided him with a reminder of who *his* 'ultimate power' was. Len's last action was more secular, as he shouted,

"Cape Canaveral here we come! Get ready, you Martians, Captain Compton and Navigator Wilby are on their way."

It was eight-fifteen on a warm August evening with many holidaymakers still strolling on the promenade and children catching the sun's last rays on the beach.

The boys' transmigratory bodies hadn't travelled such a distance on earth before, and at first, when they next reformed, both ghosts were slightly bemused by their new location, both having assumed that they would be actually in or on an unmanned space capsule, no matter how small it might be.

"Where the heck are we?" asked Len.

Eddie looked around him and said, almost sarcastically,

"On a beach, mate."

"Where's Cape Canaveral, then?"

Eddie grinned at his friend.

"Haven't you opened your eyes or something, yet?"

Len raised his eyes from the beach and looked inland.

"Oh yeah! Quite big, isn't it?"

The Titan rocket towered into the air in front of them, despite Eddie's guess that it had to be about a mile inland. He tried also to guess the local time.

"I think Florida is five hours behind us, Len."

"So if our journey here was almost instantaneous," continued Len, "it's about half past three now and we have nearly two hours to get there."

"I'm not sure, Len," replied Eddie, cautiously. "It feels and looks later, if the sun sets in Florida at about the same time as in England."

"So what do we do?" said Len.

"Well, since we didn't go direct to the launch site, I suspect we have to make our own way there – another test, I guess."

"What – we walk?"

"Can you see another way? We can hardly thumb a lift and there certainly isn't any public transport out here – it looks barren and deserted."

"Everybody's gone to watch the launch, I suppose," said Len.

"Come on", said Eddie, "there looks like a road over there."

The two ghosts glided up the white sandy beach to a wide concrete road which seemed to run in a straight line in the direction of the rocket. Len read a small sign at its start.

"Washington Avenue."

Suddenly, in front of them, they saw billowing white smoke rise in an enormous cloud above the ground, to be followed a moment later by an almost deafening roar which even their ghostly ears couldn't miss.

"Whoops, she's taking off," said Len.

"No, probably just testing the engines. I don't think space rockets take off immediately the engines first fire, but we'd better run and fast, mate."

"Come on, then," said Len, "let's run."

If the two ghosts had possessed normal human frailties, their ears would have been given a severe testing by the time they had covered about half the distance to the rocket site. They crossed over a junction, ignoring the several policemen and military personnel who were preventing traffic getting too close to the launch and, following a smaller road, strangely called Church Lane, they soon reached the more aptly named Astronaut's Boulevard. They now found themselves less than 200 yards from the launch pad and on a very wide road that actually seemed to be more like a runway. Passing through security fences and up and down bunker-like embankments, they reached their initial goal in less than five minutes. It was clear to the two boys that take-off was imminent as the voice over the public loudspeaker indicated.

"*T minus 3 minutes and counting. All systems are looking good.*"

"Now what?" asked Len as they stood on top of what appeared to be the last fire-safety embankment surrounding the launch pad. "We'll be incinerated if we go down there."

Below them was a massive concrete circle that was fifty-foot high in white noxious smoke. The flames that were shooting sideways from the rocket engines reached almost halfway to their vantage point.

"Oh don't be so dumb, Len – we can't get hurt, but that's not our real problem, mate."

"*T minus 2 minutes and counting.*"

"And that is?"

Neither boy had really noticed that they were holding a perfectly normal conversation. They barely seemed to notice the noise from the rocket's engines.

"How we get to whatever's on top of the rocket," replied Eddie as he pointed skywards. "And then how we get in."

"We have to think our way there and hope it works," said Len. "We haven't been brought all this way just for the sideshow."

"*T minus 60 seconds and counting.*"

Eddie looked sternly at his fellow ghost and said,

"We don't hope, Len; we pray, and now. So for God's sake, pray!"

"*T minus 50 seconds and counting.*"

Eddie and Len bowed their heads and prayed, and each in their own way.

"*T minus 20 seconds and counting.*"

Len couldn't concentrate on his own supplication and said,

"Nothing's happening, Eddie – it's not working."

Eddie didn't respond as he continued with his prayer until the boys' world was suddenly plunged into darkness. The sound of the final countdown began to fade from their hearing.

"*… nine … eight … seven … six … all engines at maximum power … three … two … one … zero. We have lift-off. Viking One is go!*"

In earth time it was to be another ten months before the two ghosts became aware of anything new. On June the 19th 1976, Eddie and Len had their first 'close-up' view of the Red Planet, albeit from over 2000 kilometres above its surface. They had woken from their sleep to find themselves sitting on a very peculiar spacecraft. The orbiter had certainly not been designed to carry humans, and though its shape was immaterial for the transport of two ghosts, it was an odd experience for them as they sat, each on two wing-like structures that protruded from the main body of the instrument-carrying craft. This time, Len had pre-empted his friend by making the security check from his position a short distance away. In his excitement at the discovery of their new environment, Eddie had forgotten to do the usual verification of his friend's identity.

With small engines to correct the tilt of the spacecraft, the Mars orbiter also carried the lander that would eventually be ejected to the surface of the planet. Both ghosts spent some time after the identity checks studying which part of their spacecraft *was* the lander and, more importantly, how they would get in or on it. It didn't look obvious to them how they would land.

For the next month, the two ghosts watched each other from a distance of a few feet, fixed in a curious state of inertia, neither able to move nor speak. To make their existence even stranger, the powers of thought and sight were *not* denied them, and for the next thirty-three earth days they could do nothing more than study the planet's surface from distances varying between two and fifty thousand kilometres. Though they had been given a privilege that was beyond all but the characters from a science fiction novel, it was initially mentally and psychologically tiring and a kind of a living torture, even for their ghostly minds and souls.

On July the 20th, by earth time, things started to change for the two ghosts. Firstly, their ability to move and speak returned and secondly noises could suddenly be heard from the main body of the orbiter.

"Wh-what's that?" shouted Len. Eddie shrugged his shoulders as both boys stood upright and walked towards the middle of the weird looking craft. Unlike the probable reaction of normal beings, neither ghost felt much after-effect from their static ordeal. Indeed, their memories of it seem to fade quickly as they began to realise that something important was about to take place.

"I bet that's the orbiter beginning its separation, so that the lander can drop down to the surface," replied Eddie. "It sounds like some retrorockets have been fired to slow the whole thing down before separation. Look down, Len – we're much closer now."

Len glanced down and saw that Mars no longer had any curvature. They were so close that it appeared flat and covered by dust clouds, some of which they were passing through at that moment in their low orbit. They could only get brief glimpses of the surface below.

"I checked before and I think we'll have to get on that thing below us," said Eddie. "I think that must be the lander."

"And just how do you suggest we get down there? We can't jump – nothing would happen if we did, and we don't have the ability to hold on to anything, anyway," said Len. "Do we pray again?"

"No, I think there's a way that we can get onto the lander. Look, see down there – there are some footholds below us on the side of the orbiter. We just step down onto the first one and as long as we keep one foot in contact with something, we should be alright. It doesn't look more than three or four feet."

The rockets were sounding louder now and without waiting for his friend to reply, Eddie took a step onto the first foothold. Len watched as he then removed his other foot from the orbiter and second later, Eddie was on the lander. However, 'on the lander' was a poor description for his final position. With no flat surface to sit or stand on, he seemed to be hovering just above the complicated array of instruments which the lander mainly consisted of. Quickly, Len copied his friend's manoeuvre and joined him in a similar position and orientation.

"We're not in contact with it, Eddie," said a bewildered Len.

"No, I know, but we're going with it, I think."

Suddenly, the boys looked to their right to see the orbiter disappearing into the distance. Such was the separation speed; it was out of view in less than a second. Below them, more rockets fired as the lander prepared to come out of orbit and into the planet's atmosphere. For nearly three hours, the two ghosts chatted happily to each other as the lander was slowed in preparation for its landing. Soon, three huge parachutes were deployed and after a few more seconds, three legs were extended to form a tripod beneath the vital collection of instruments. Less than two minutes later the lander arrived on Mars with a relatively light jolt. The two ghosts felt nothing as they just seemed to slide off the lander and onto the Martian surface. Standing up, both boys dwarfed the lander and its bundle of instruments, cameras and scientific experiments by a couple of feet. Their eleven-month space ride was finally over, and they found once again that they were able to walk and even dance normally on the Martian surface, unhindered by the lack of any usual sustainer of human life. Len even shouted his own greeting.

"Martians, we come in peace as the first beings from earth to visit your planet. We come for all mankind."

They were soon to discover, however, that Len's claim to exclusivity was totally mistaken and unwarranted.

16

Universal Evil

Len's carefree attitude to his new environment seemed to know no bounds, as he jogged up and down for a hundred yards or so in every direction surveying the barren and eerie landscape. A Martian twilight had descended on a tundra-like and featureless plain of reddish-grey dirt and rocks. Overhead, a thin grey mist cloaked the Martian surface, forming a ceiling as low as twenty feet. Patches of white frost dotted the landscape indicating the temperature of the boys' hostile surroundings. Eddie did his best to ignore his fellow ghost's over-eagerness to explore what lay beyond their immediate horizon by remaining near to the lander and inspecting its apparatus that occasionally whirred into life. In the end a few chosen words brought Len back down to earth.

"Stop a minute, Len!" he shouted as his friend was passing the lander on another of his short scouting missions. "Just slow down, will you. I want to talk to you."

Len trotted back to the lander, his enthusiasm obviously still close to fever pitch.

"What's up, Captain? I want to go and find some Martians. You can't be tired, surely?"

"No, I don't feel tired, Len; I'm just a bit disorientated, I suppose."

Eddie paused for a moment and then said,

"You do realise something, don't you?"

"What, mate?"

"You do know that, despite what we said about wanting to explore the universe, we have no apparent means of leaving this planet. I think you'll agree that, from what you've seen already, it looks pretty boring up here, and are you really sure you would never want to go back to earth, either?"

Len went quiet and the sudden silence seemed to have a hollow ring to it, making their new world even eerier than before. It wasn't long, however, before he tried to lighten the mood.

"We'll just have to go and find the Martian equivalent of Cape Canaveral and go on a mission."

Then Len paused and, after a moment, he said,

"But seriously though, we knew that before we set off. I'm not going to miss anything back on earth – are you?"

"I don't know, Len. I agree – back in Fenton it all seemed so boring – the excitement had started to wane, but this doesn't look much better, does it?"

"Death is what you make it, Captain."

The doubts that Eddie had articulated about the finality of their new situation had been actually nothing more than an expression of his own concerns and worries. There was no question that Len's characteristic bravado had helped him ease his anxieties, but as the two ghosts set off to investigate the Red Planet, Eddie was still unsure where their so-called 'last mission' was taking them and, indeed, what they would find when they had completed it.

Len was typically jovial as they walked away from the busy lander, remarking on the camera that was snapping photographs behind them.

"We'll be on the front pages in a few days; I wish I'd combed my hair."

With Eddie half-expecting the lander to start moving on its three legs and follow them, he broke into a trot with Len calling out,

"Hold on, Captain – what's the rush? We've got the rest of our deaths!"

Eddie glanced back as his friend caught up with him. He looked past Len at the lander, now some fifty yards distant, and he had the distinct impression that the camera was still trained on them, as if it was following their every move. His musing was quickly broken by his friend.

"Not so fast, mate – are you sure we're going in the right direction?"

"What right direction? Everywhere looks the same to me."

"Not over there, Eddie," replied Len, pointing at the horizon to their left. "Seems to be brighter there."

Eddie looked to where his friend was indicating, and at first, he struggled to make out any difference in the horizon. After his eyes had refocused on the distant line, however, he suddenly saw what Len meant. Rather than a general lifting of the Martian twilight across the whole horizon, the brightness seemed to be coming from a concentrated source.

"Someone's shining a torch," said Len.

"Don't be daft," replied Eddie.

"Well, it's not a fixed light. Look – it's moving from side to side."

Eddie said nothing. His eyes now were fixed rigidly on the light which was getting brighter and closer by the second. It got to a position about a hundred yards away before Len said excitedly,

"It's on the ground – it's rolling along the ground."

The two ghosts watched, mesmerised as a ball of light, the size of a football rolled towards them on the red dirt surface. It was powerful enough to brighten the surrounding area for a distance up to thirty yards in any direction. It came to within a few feet of the astonished ghosts and stopped. The light seemed to have a fluorescent quality, illuminating the ground with a blue-green radiance. Len seemed to be less fearful than his friend and, while Eddie watched open-mouthed, he walked calmly towards the ball of light, his foot getting to within a few inches of it before it suddenly backed away on its original path to stop again after about ten yards. The two ghosts waited. Then the ball of light moved forward again and this time it came to rest right in front of them. Len took aim to 'kick' it with his right foot and Eddie shouted,

"Stop it, Len! You don't what it might do."

Sensing Len's intention, the ball instantly moved to its left and back again, the oscillation taking less than a second. Like something out of a computer game, it then proceeded to dance and weave left and right, as if to say: '*Catch me if you can*!' Eddie relaxed and smiled. The light seemed friendly enough and wanted to have some fun. As soon as Len then withdrew his foot, the light ceased its crazy dance and backed away again.

"What's it doing?" asked Len.

The ball came forward once more and Eddie and Len watched as the process was repeated, the ball backing further away each time. Eddie then seemed to guess what it was doing.

"I think it wants us to follow it, Len."

To try and test out his theory, Eddie walked forward to within a couple of feet of the ball. After a pause, it backed away again and stopped. Len joined his friend.

"You seem to be correct," said Len. "But the question is: Why?"

"Don't know, mate – it obviously wants to take us somewhere or show us something. We might as well follow it and find out."

The ghosts walked forward together and all at once the light did a strange hop into the air before continuing on its backward path.

"It's happy now," said Len. "It's just nodded to us that we should follow it."

The light continued on its path towards the horizon for more than half an hour, if the boys had been able to measure it in earth time. If they got too far behind, it would wait until they were within twenty yards or so and continue – thus keeping them in its circle of illumination and guiding them safely forward.

With nothing to gauge time, it was impossible for the two ghosts to estimate how far they had walked when the light came to an abrupt halt in front of them. Eddie had picked a point on the original horizon when they had set off, but they had soon passed it and the process was repeated several times more before the ball of light stopped. Though tiredness was not an issue, boredom certainly was.

"What now?" asked Len. "I'm getting fed up with this."

"Maybe it has forgotten where it is," replied Eddie.

"Oh yeah? I somehow doubt it, mate."

Eddie didn't think so, either, as he had formed a strange feeling that the light was just checking on its followers' welfare. Suddenly, the ball started to move again, but this time, at right angles to its original path. The two boys turned to their right to follow it and within a few hundred yards, the scenery started to change. The Martian surface was now criss-crossed by a series of ravines, some shallow and some impossibly deep to the boys' ghostly eyes in the dim light. Without their guiding light, one or both of them might have walked into one of the gorges, even though their innate ability to float would have probably saved them from disappearing completely into the bowels of the planet. Soon, their tortuous trail led them on a slow descent into their own ravine, flanked on both sides by sheer rock faces of unknown height. As their route became narrower, tiny balls of light appeared to line each side of their path, where, even at Martian midday, very little natural light would ever reach. Their friendly ball suddenly had a double array of junior companions forming a guard of honour for the two ghosts' progress. Eddie was becoming nervous.

"I don't like this, Len. Looks like we're expected."

"Just laying out the red carpet for their earthly visitors, I think, mate," replied Len, almost casually. "They won't have seen the likes of us before – I'm game to see their leader."

"You think that's what's happening? We're being taken to their leader?"

"What else could it be?"

The light ahead of them had suddenly stopped again. It waited while the ghosts caught up after their brief conversation. As Eddie and Len approached, it seemed to grow brighter and the extra light was concentrated all in one direction at an angle to their path, illuminating what looked to be a deep hole or shaft. Reaching the very edge of the hole, they could see that a flight of rock steps led downwards in a spiral staircase that seemed to have no foot. The ball of light joined them at the top of the hole. Shrinking in size, it bounced its way down the first few steps and waited.

"It wants us to go down there?" queried a nervous Eddie.

"In for a penny, in for a pound," replied his friend. "Come on, let's go."

Len descended the first three steps. The light descended three more and stopped again. Reluctantly, Eddie followed, and a few steps at a time, the two ghosts slowly made their way down the rock staircase, turning through 360 degrees on so many occasions that Eddie lost count. Towards the bottom of their descent, the light in front of them began to fade as more permanent and static light from below filtered upwards. Reaching the last few steps, their 'friendly' guide disappeared completely and their path opened up into an enormous cavern on an Egyptian pyramid scale.

Len's reaction was predictable.

"Wow!"

The two ghosts walked forward into a roughly hemispherical chamber, whose diameter had to be at least the length of a football pitch. Stone staircases, similar to the one they had just descended, spiralled upwards from three other positions on the circumference of the cavern, which in turn was brilliantly lit by a huge ball of light, floating near the top of the chamber's ceiling. Smaller balls illuminated the staircases and marked the very edge of the arena. It was both a magnificent and frightening sight for the two human ghosts.

"So where are the Martians, then?" asked Len, looking round the massive chamber. There was no sign of any movement on the cavern floor, which was composed of flat, bare rock. Apart from some places where the rock was so shiny it reflected flashes of the unnatural fluorescent light, the floor was completely devoid of any defining features. The boys had by now reached the centre of the enormous chamber and, standing back-to-back, they gazed at its distant edges.

"There can't be anyone here, Len," replied Eddie after a while.

"Depends what you mean by, anyone."

"What do you mean?" asked Eddie.

"I mean, we have no idea what things look like on Mars. For all we know, those lights might be the inhabitants of this place – the one that brought us here seemed alive enough to me. It appeared to know what we were doing."

The two ghosts swapped positions and studied the cavern some more. The boys' conversation echoed off the sloping rock walls in their silent surroundings. Eddie seemed to be disturbed by the noise, but Len was getting impatient.

"I wonder what would happen if we just climbed back up the way we came. Would anyone or anything would try to stop us, do you think?"

Eddie, sensing danger, said,

"Don't try it, Len. I'm sure we haven't been brought all this way just to be sent back the way we've come."

"You mean we're prisoners here?"

"No, not exactly prisoners, but we are guests of whoever has brought us here. Remember, we're visitors to this planet."

"Well, they're not treating us like guests – keeping us waiting like this."

Rather than approach the staircase they had come in by, Len walked casually over to the one that was diametrically opposite to it. Eddie waited nervously in the middle of the chamber, issuing a note of caution as he did so.

"Be careful, Len."

Len reached the foot of the staircase and peered up into the black hole that enclosed it.

"Nothing here," he shouted. "It's just like the other one."

Len's voice caused such a disturbing echo that even he took a step backwards as it reverberated round the cavern. The echo bothered Eddie and he called to Len to return to the chamber's centre.

"Something's not quite right, Len," he said.

"What?"

"It's the echo."

"What about it?"

"I don't think we should be able to make an echo – we're ghosts after all."

"Why not?"

"Because our voices aren't real and we're imaginary beings, so how can we make sounds that echo off something that is real, like the rock walls. It doesn't make sense to me."

"So, perhaps we're the only things that can hear the echoes," said Len with some disinterest in his friend's apparent conundrum. "After all, we can hear each other's voices, so why not their echoes?"

"Because if our voices create sound waves that solid walls can reflect, then those same sound waves could be heard by living beings as well. No?"

"You may be right, Mr Compton, but you'll never know, will you, because there are no living beings down here, my dear – only us."

The new voice echoed around the underground chamber, but nothing was visible to either boy to suggest its source.

"What the …?" muttered Len.

"Stay still!" shouted Eddie as suddenly the overhead ball of light swung to its left lighting up one of the staircases. Slowly, figures came into view from the bottom of the stairs. First, one, then another and finally a third black-robed 'being' strode into the arena, like gladiators into a coliseum. The leader threw back his black hood and approached the quivering ghosts.

"Hello, my dears and how are we today? Surprised to see me, no doubt."

Eddie had recognised the sycophantic voice almost immediately he had heard it from the staircase as Len did now.

"Oh my God, it's old Granty!" he exclaimed.

"Yes, Leonard Wilby and Edward Compton, it is I, Aloyisious St John Grant, late of Fenton-on-Sea and former proprietor of The Emporium on Steep Hill that bore my name. I understand it's been turned into some tearooms now. What a shame. I do believe I met your sister there some time ago, young Eddie, and what's more – I saw her boyfriend propose to her."

"Yes, I know, Ally – she told me."

"Really?"

Though Len had always been uneasy with old Granty's effeminate ways, he was brave enough to say,

"What are you doing here, Mr Grant, then?"

"Oh, Leonard, my dear – please call me Ally like your nice young friend does. We don't stand on ceremony down here."

Len and Eddie cast glances behind Aloyisious Grant at his two companions, neither of whom had removed their black cowls. Eddie, for one, knew that all was definitely not well. The last time they had seen old Granty's ghost he had seemed normal with a pleasant and caring attitude. This version of him spoke in a creepy and sarcastic tone. Eddie knew what that meant and his friend had sensed it, too.

"Your Ally's evil ghost, aren't you," said Len. "And who are the people behind you?"

"Evil? I'm not evil, Leonard Wilby. Whatever gave you that impression? No, my dear boys, I'm here to help you two travellers – show you the ropes, you know. You've done well to get here and now you need some advice and assistance if you're to pass to the next level. You won't believe what I can do for you."

Len said nothing as Eddie noticed a faint smile begin to form on his friend's face. Ally Grant continued.

"Let me you show you my two friends. I know you're both dying to know who they are. I suspect they will be familiar to you. Step forward, friend!"

The first cloaked and hooded figure moved to stand on Ally's right.

"This is my first assistant, so to speak."

The black hood was thrown backwards in a show of pomp and ceremony. Eddie gasped.

"George? Is it really you, George?"

"Of course it is, Eddie, my friend – your old ally and fellow adventurer, George Canter."

"Mr Canter?" stammered Len in disbelief.

"Yes, Len, and please call me George."

"Sorry, George."

Ally smiled knowingly and turning to the final hooded figure, he said,

"Step forward, friend!"

As before, the figure move forward and flamboyantly threw back his hood.

"Mr Manders!" exclaimed Len.

"Hello, Len and Eddie. It's nice to see you both."

'So, here they all are', thought Eddie, 'three characters from his and Len's past, both real and imagined; three men of vastly different characters and backgrounds; three men, whose lives spanned a century and a half, but also three ghosts who were, each and every one, evil – pure evil'. But Len was not as sure and remarked,

"It's good to see you all again. We wondered why we'd been brought here."

"Shut up, Len! Don't get involved. Don't be deceived by them."

George Canter looked genuinely shocked at Eddie's reaction.

"I told you, Eddie, it is me. Why don't you believe me?"

"You don't quite look right to me."

"Look right? How should I look?"

"I don't know – just different."

Ally Grant interrupted the debate.

"Don't I look and sound the same, Eddie, my dear?"

"Or me?" echoed Jacob Manders and then even Len realised the truth of the matter as the three ghosts chanted in unison.

"*How should we look? How should we look?*"

"*Who shall we be? Who shall we be?*"

Suddenly, as if to make the point and demonstrate their power, the three ghosts covered their heads with their hoods. They remained motionless for a few seconds and then threw back their hood s again.

Both boys gasped in astonishment when they realised that all three ghosts had interchanged their heads. George's body was surmounted by Jacob's head; Jacob's body by Ally's head and Ally's body by George's head. A new chant started.

"*Who are we now, boys? Who are we now, boys?*"

As Eddie and Len watched in horror, the process was repeated again and again until Eddie shouted,

"You're all evil! Go to the devil! Get thee behind me, Satan!"

"*Go to the devil! Go to the devil!*"

Eddie's incantation wasn't working – the evil ghosts weren't going anywhere. Eddie tried again.

"Oh God, rid us of this evil before us, I pray thee."

"*I pray thee. I pray thee,*" the ghosts chanted.

"It's not working, Eddie. Their power is too strong."

"Good can always defeat evil," shouted Eddie as the chanting got more rhythmic and louder.

"Well, it's not beating this evil," shouted Len above the incessant noise. "We'll have to make a run for it."

Len turned to run for their entry staircase, but he hadn't gone more than a few yards when his legs suddenly ceased moving and his body became frozen in space. The three black-robed figures advanced towards him. Eddie sank to his knees and prayed.

"Please save Len. Please save him."

Ally Grant got to within a couple of feet when Len's body broke its invisible shackles and Len fled to the bottom of the staircase. Eddie then lost sight of him as he disappeared into the blackness of the exit shaft. Muttering more prayers to himself, Eddie got off his knees and bolted after his friend. Behind him he heard more rhythmic chanting.

"*Come and join us*! *Come and join us*!"

"*We will get you*! *We will get you*!"

"*Just you wait and see*! *Just you wait and see*!"

Eddie didn't wait and he wasn't stopped like his friend. He made it to the staircase. It was black, pitch black and he could hear Len above him.

"I can't see, oh, I can't see. Where are you, Eddie?"

"I'm here, Len. Just stay where you are."

Eddie prayed again. Len shouted,

"It's getting lighter. I can see. Quick, Eddie!"

For the next few minutes and with just a few feet separating them, the two boys bounded up the spiral staircase, guided by the unknown light source above them. Len waited at the top of the shaft until Eddie emerged once again into the narrow ravine. The light source had moved a long way ahead of them by this time, providing only a dim target to make their escape complete. The gentle incline which led there was now in darkness – all the tiny lights had disappeared, no longer providing a guide to the chamber of evil.

17

Mind Talk

Not until the two ghosts had reached the top of the narrow ravine, following the dim and distant guiding light, were they ready to stop and discuss their experience of evil. With the latticework of deep gorges immediately in front of them, it was time also to consider their next move – neither wanted to face the possibility of sliding or falling into another ravine. The Martian night had taken over completely and even Eddie was unsure how long it would last.

"We could be in darkness for days if we stay here, you know."

"You mean day and night are not the same as back on earth?" asked Len, somewhat surprised.

"I don't honestly know what the difference is, but it's not going to be the same."

Both ghosts had seemed to want to talk about anything else but their recent experience until Eddie then suddenly said quietly,

"Were you nearly fooled by those three ghosts, Len?"

Len didn't respond straightaway and Eddie continued.

"Because, if you did think they were Ally's, George's and Jacob's good ghosts, just remember that evil attracts evil – good is an individual thing."

"No, I don't suppose I was really fooled. I just can't understand how three such nice men could have anything evil about them. I mean, apart from old Granty's effeminate and ingratiating manner, they were all thoughtful and caring men – at least one of them saved our lives. Even though old Granty was weird, he wouldn't hurt a fly in real life."

The light in the distance had all but disappeared by now and the two ghosts had difficulty seeing each other's faces. The mist overhead seemed to have thickened, too, as Eddie replied,

"Everyone has an evil side, mate. Look at you for example; I seemed to remember you pulling a nasty stunt in Fenton with my little nephew. What matters in the end is not giving in to it as a permanent choice."

"I never see your evil side very often, Eddie, except …."

"Except?"

"Except when you think you know it all and try to tell me how I should behave. Thinking you're always good and always right is evil too, isn't it?"

Eddie seemed reluctant to reply – he knew his friend had highlighted his biggest failing: pride.

"Yes, I know I'm evil, Len, but I am trying to do something about it."

"There you go again – showing off," said Len.

It was clear to both boys that an argument was about to ensue and sensing it, Eddie tried to be more humble, as he said,

"Sorry, Len – I don't mean to always sound smug and self-satisfied; I just want to make sure neither of us ends up in the wrong place where evil reigns supreme."

"You mean …?"

"Yes, you can say it, Len – hell."

It was pitch-black now and with the mist descending to ground level, the visibility was virtually down to zero. Len was anxious to be moving.

"I want to get out of here, Eddie."

"And how do you propose we do that? We can't even see to move an inch."

"Only one way, Captain," replied Len. "We have to think our way out again."

"So, where do you want to go?"

"Anywhere that's a long way from this evil place."

Eddie thought for a moment and said, almost jokingly,

"How about infinity, or just the edge of the universe, as we know it?"

"Edge of the known universe will do me, mate. I'm not so sure about infinity. I don't think such a place exists."

"O.K., Commander Armstrong – the edge it is. Maybe we'll discover extra-terrestrial life there."

"Good," said Len. "We can go and haunt some little green men who've got two heads."

"As long as you don't try and pull any evil stunts again – O.K?"

Eddie didn't see the evil grin that had appeared on his friend's face. It was to be an invisible pointer to some future sorrow.

"O.K.," replied Len after a split-second pause.

In the blackness, neither ghost dared move their position as they concentrated their minds on their next space journey. While Eddie's avid reading of science fiction books and magazines presented him with some relevant images to think about, his friend struggled to imagine anything other than scenes similar to the Martian landscape. After a short time, Eddie broke the silence with,

"We're going to have to try something different, Len. This isn't working."

"You try praying, then – I'm still not sure God listens to me."

Eddie resisted the temptation to tell his friend he had to really believe before his prayers would work, given their earlier conversation. He didn't want to appear arrogant and superior as Len had suggested. Though there would be no difference in his vision, Eddie shut his eyes and prayed. Suddenly, through closed eyelids, he sensed the blackness had lifted slightly. Len immediately whispered,

"The lights are back on again. What did you do?"

"I hadn't really started," said Eddie as he looked backwards to see the dual strip of tiny ball-lights was illuminating the narrow ravine leading back to the chamber of evil. Len was standing further away from him than he had imagined and Eddie shouted an immediate warning.

"For God's sake, don't step backwards, mate. Walk forward slowly."

Len realised from his friends' tone that he must be on the edge of one of the many deep slits in the ground and, without looking back, he walked forward gingerly.

"Without realising it, you must have started to walk when you said you wanted to leave this place," said Eddie.

The lights behind them seemed to be burning brighter now and it then hit Eddie what might be about to happen.

"We'd better get out of here, Len."

"That's what we were trying to do, I thought, Captain."

Suddenly, noises broke from the ravine behind them, and they were rhythmic again.

"*We're coming to get you! We're coming to get you!*"

"*You belong to us! You belong to us!*"

For some strange reason, Eddie and Len seemed to be rooted to the spot, unable to move a muscle. The chanting stopped abruptly. The three black figures came into view about fifty yards down the sloping ramp. George, Jacob and Ally hadn't given up their quest for the boys' souls. Though the chanting had stopped, Eddie could hear their muttered conversation as it echoed off the steep sides of the ravine. It was too indistinct to determine individual voices and, in any case, back in the chamber they had all begun to sound the same.

"That Eddie Compton thinks he's too good for us; it'll be hard to persuade him to join us."

"Yes, but Mr Leonard Wilby would like to be one of us, I think. His soul seems sometimes to be in tune with our beliefs. We may get him quite easily."

By the look on Len's face, now dimly lit by the tiny lights, it was clear to Eddie that his friend had heard little or any of the evil ghosts' threatening words. The chanting started up again with the three black-hooded figures less than ten yards away.

"We want you, Leonard Wilby! *We want you, Leonard Wilby!"*

"Come and join us! *Come and join us!"*

Suddenly, the evil troop stopped their advance – changing quickly from Indian file to a line of three abreast the narrow path. The middle figure took a step forward. He spoke softly with an intonation that was a curious mixture of all three of the ghosts' voices.

"Come, boys, we mean you no harm. We want you to have fun, and you can, if you join us. You like playing tricks, don't you, Leonard?"

"Sometimes."

"Well, we do tricks beyond your wildest imagination. We can make people do things. What do you say, young Wilby?"

"Say nothing," said Eddie quickly, before his friend could reply. He and Len were still transfixed and unable to move. The three black figures moved forward as one. Eddie fell to his knees and held two fingers up in the sign of the cross; the only thing he hadn't thought of trying until then. Suddenly, the lights in the ravine started going out one by one. Eddie held his finger cross firm and the first figure fell to the ground in a cloud of dust and white vapour; to be followed quickly by the second and third in similar manner. Mobility immediately returned to the boys' ethereal bodies and they found themselves able to walk forward to the fallen men. With very little light to show them the way, they reached the spot where the three evil ghosts had stood to find they had literally disappeared 'in a puff of smoke'. Len then turned to Eddie and said,

"Now, for God's sake, get us out of here!"

As Len, almost unwittingly, made his plea for divine intervention, the final light suddenly shone brighter, allowing each boy to see the other's face in eerie and gaunt detail. They were given this dubious privilege for no more than a few brief seconds before utter blackness returned to that part of the Martian surface. Little did either boy know, but that was to be the last time they would ever be able to see each other's face again.

To all intents and purposes, it was to be irrelevant how long the two ghosts would be in peaceful oblivion after their excursion to Mars. Whether it was a few minutes or several million years was of no consequence when they finally 'awoke'. In fact, neither boy could really tell if they were awake, or indeed, when such an event had happened. They each discovered quickly that they could hardly even call themselves ghosts, let alone boys, any longer. Once before they had been deprived of physical, albeit ghostly, movement, but their new situation paled that into insignificance. Now, neither boy possessed the power of hearing, speech or sight – they were deaf, dumb and blind. Though it was stating the obvious – without sight, they could not see each other; without hearing, they could not hear each other and without speech, they could even not tell each other about their first two handicaps. Even if they had been able to see, there would have been nothing of their bodies to be seen. In short, they were without shape or form, bereft of everything except for one small, but important faculty – they still possessed their minds. This was the one sense in which they could still call themselves 'beings' – they could think and, unlike that tragic part of the human race who were also lacking in the three most vital senses, they would soon find they could exchanges their thoughts between each other as well. Eddie would have argued that they had souls as well which, together with their powers of thought, still set them apart from animals of a lower class.

Given all of this, it was also clearly irrelevant where they were in space and time, or even whether they were both in the *same* place and in the *same* time. Indeed, since they couldn't occupy space anyway, the idea didn't even seem to warrant consideration. They had reached the ultimate level in their development, no longer even able to wander invisibly through the universe, or to impinge on any human being's psyche. Their existence was solely defined by and encapsulated in their own minds and their ability to think. Their desire to reach the distant parts of the cosmos had been thwarted at the last moment.

The 'conversation' took some time to get started as both boys' minds struggled to cope with their own internal machinations. It wasn't until 'Len' began thinking of his friend that the thought transference began. It was a stumbling beginning as both minds tussled with and sifted out snippets of extraneous suggestions. If either mind had been able to convert its thoughts into a verbal or written communication, the following would have been a good representation.

'*I wonder where Eddie is.*'

'*Nowhere – where are you?*'

'*The same.*'

'*Did you get to the edge of the universe?*'

'*Don't know – this might be it.*'

'*Are we awake?*'

'*Can't tell.*'

'*Can you feel or see anything?*'

'*No – can you?*'

'*No.*'

'*I think I must be dead.*'

'*You already were.*'

'*Is this real death, now?*'

'*Don't know.*'

'*What's the capital of England?*'

'*London. Why?*'

'*Just checking.*'

'*What's my name?*'

'*Edward Compton. What's mine?*'

'*Leonard Wilby. Are you being good, Leonard Wilby?*'

'*Can't do anything else.*'

'*What thoughts have you had?*'

'*I want to go to sleep.*'

'*Have you had any bad thoughts, Len?*'

'*Yes.*'

'*What were they?*'

'*Can't tell you – they're evil.*'

'*I just got them anyway while you were thinking of them.*'

'*Oh yeah – what were they?*'

'*You want to go and join the black ghosts.*'

'*How did you know that?*'

'*I told you – I read you.*'

'*I want to go. I want to go.*'

'*Well, go then.*'

'*Come with me.*'

'*No, Len.*'

'*We'd get our senses back.*'

'*How do you know that?*'

'*Ally told me.*'

'*When?*'

'*Just now.*'

'*How?*'

'*Same way you knew I wanted to go.*'

'*You're swapping thoughts?*'

'*Yes – you don't have exclusivity.*'

'*He's evil.*'

'*No, I'm not, Edward.*'

'*Don't go, Len.*'

'*Do go, Len.*'

'*I may do. What can you offer me, Ally?*'

'*Your invisible body back.*'

'*He's lying.*'

'*Am I?*'

'*Go away, Satan!*'

'*I'm bored with this, Eddie.*'

'*Just think of some nice things.*'

'*Like what?*'

'*Things you always wanted to do. Imagine playing football for England.*'

'*Mm – that's nice.*'

'*What else?*'

'*Think of your mum.*'

'*Mm – that's nice.*'

'*What else?*'

'*Imagine you're in heaven.*'

'*What does that mean?*'

'*You'll be happy and be able to see everyone again.*'

'*Are you in heaven, Eddie?*'

'*Don't know.*'

'*Do you want to go to heaven, Eddie?*'

'*Yes – do you?*'

'*Don't know.*'

'*Remember when we went on holiday to Ludmouth?*'

'*Mm – that's nice.*'

'*Remember when you scored the winning goal in the inter-school cup final?*'

'*Mm – that's nice.*'

'*Remember when we went to Poland on our fantastic journey?*'

'*Mm – that was exciting.*'

'*That's heaven, Len.*'

'*What? I do not understand.*'

'*Heaven is anything you want it to be – anything that makes you feel happy.*'

'*So, am I in heaven?*'

'*Don't know.*'

'*You don't want to go to heaven. Come with us.*'

'*Go away, Ally.*'

'*It's not Ally, Eddie – it's your old friend George.*'

'*Ugh*!'

'*Would I lead you into trouble, Eddie?*'

'*Yes – you're evil.*'

'*Am I?*'

'*Ye-es.*'

'*You don't sound sure, Eddie.*'

'*Come on, Captain, let's go and join George.*'

'*Come on, Eddie. Come on, Eddie. Come on, Eddie.*'

'*You only have to think of it and we'll make it happen for you.*'

'*I'm going, Eddie. I don't want to stay like this forever.*'

'*Come on, Eddie. Come on, Eddie. Come on, Eddie.*'

'*I don't want to go to …, Eddie. I want to go to ….*'

'*Please, God, save me!*'

18
Limbo

And then …?

www.ingramcontent.com/pod-product-compliance
Lightning Source LLC
Chambersburg PA
CBHW051130020726
47501CB00005B/1439

* 9 7 8 0 9 5 5 9 8 7 2 2 9 *